Beate Teresa Hanika

Learning to Scream

Translated by Katy Derbyshire

First published in German in 2009
by S. Fischer Verlay GmbH

This English edition first published in 2010 by
ANDERSEN PRESS LIMITED
20 Vauxhall Bridge Road
London SW1V 2SA
www.andersenpress.co.uk

Copyright © S. Fischer Verlay GmbH, Frankfurt, Main, 2009
Translation © Katy Derbyshire, 2010

British Library Cataloguing in Publication Data available.

The translation of this work was supported by a grant from the
Goethe-Institut which is funded by the German Ministry of Foreign Affairs.

ISBN 978 184 939 060 6

Typesetting by FiSH Books, Enfield
Printed and bound in Great Britain by CPI Bookmarque, Croydon CR0 4TD

For Flo

My name's Malvina. I'll be fourteen on the first of May. It's April now.

That's two weeks to go. When I'm fourteen I'm going to have a boyfriend. I'll hold his hand and he'll hold me in his arms. I'll go to parties and dance, even if my parents say no. I'll always say what I think and I'll get angry, not sad. I'll be able to shout so loud that everyone will be scared of me and run away whenever I want.

Even my parents, even my granddad, everyone.

It's April now, and I'm thirteen years old.

Friday

It happens on a Friday afternoon.

The last Friday before the Easter holidays.

I have to go to piano lessons every Friday. And then to my granddad's, because he lives in the same street and Dad waits for me at his flat. Sometimes my big sister Anne picks me up there, or my brother Paul, but he's six years older than me and he's at uni now, so he's not there all that often.

Mum never comes to pick me up because she can't stand Granddad, especially now Gran's dead. He's been even nastier to her since then, she says, so she doesn't visit him any more.

On this last Friday before the Easter holidays I'm really happy once my piano lesson is finally over. It's the school holidays, it's half past four in the afternoon, the sun is shining, and I pull my jumper off over my head as I cross the road – not because it's so

1

hot but because I decide it's officially springtime. I'd be even happier if Lizzy was here. Lizzy's my very best friend and she picks me up from piano every Friday. So it's not so boring round at Granddad's. We swap the latest gossip or do our homework together – OK, usually we just chat and pretend to do our homework. Lizzy's not here today because she's gone on a skiing trip straight from school. She was even allowed to leave her school an hour earlier than everyone else.

In the old days, my gran used to open the door, and on the day before the Easter holidays she'd say:

'It's the start of the ice-cream season!'

Because there was only ice cream at my gran's in the summer. Vanilla ice cream with jelly beans on top.

Since she died we've had ice cream all year round – and the funny thing is, that feels a bit sad.

But I'm not sad today, I'm in the best of moods and I ring and ring Granddad's doorbell so that everyone knows it's me and it's the holidays and I'm in a really good mood.

Granddad opens the door and says:

'Here's my Malvina, my favourite granddaughter.'

I plant a kiss on his cheek and slip past him into his flat, which always reeks of wine and old cheese because Granddad starts drinking wine at three in the afternoon, and sometimes he has cheese with it too. Disgusting cheese that he holds under my nose, laughing himself silly when I screw up my face in disgust.

Something's different today, but I don't notice it until I reach the living room.

Dad's not here.

'Where is he?' I ask.

Granddad sits down in his armchair and crosses his legs. He's got really long legs; he's over one metre ninety – I get that from him, everyone says. I'm thirteen and I'm almost one metre seventy-five already. I could do without it; I'm always taller than all the boys, and that's no fun.

'He's picking your sister up,' says Granddad, and I sit down in the armchair opposite him, slightly uncomfortable because I don't know what to talk to him about.

I haven't been on my own with him for a long time. In the old days Gran was always here, and Lizzy. Since Gran died, Dad's been taking more care of Granddad so he doesn't get lonely. They talk, mostly about the war, when my granddad was a boy, and stuff like that, and Lizzy and I sit next to them and whisper and write silly notes to each other on slips of paper.

I think about what I could ask Granddad about the war; I really can't think of anything no matter how hard I try, so I don't say anything and just hope Dad and Anne will turn up soon.

'How old are you now, Malvina?' Granddad asks, even though he knows full well I'm thirteen.

'Thirteen,' I say, still thinking about the war.

Just as I'm about to ask him what it was like, just

for the sake of asking something even though I know all about it already, he says:

'And have you got a boyfriend? Your cousin Maggie's got one, and she's only six-months older than you.'

The blood rushes to my face and I just shake my head. Of course I haven't got a boyfriend, and even if I did have one I wouldn't tell my granddad.

'You're old enough now,' he insists. 'Go on, you can tell me.'

He gives me a searching look as he says it, as if I wanted to keep something secret from him.

I start feeling more and more uncomfortable. I wish I could disappear on the spot, but I can't think of anything to say. *I forgot my music folder at the piano teacher's place* ... but my music folder's right here by my feet.

So I say, 'I really haven't got a boyfriend, Granddad.'

'I can't believe that, you're such a pretty girl, you're my prettiest granddaughter...I bet all the boys are after you, aren't they?'

I just shake my head again and look past Granddad's face out of the window, at the block of flats opposite. A woman is shaking a duster out of the window. She looks right over at me for a moment but I'm just imagining it – she couldn't possibly see me in here in the half-light. She slams the window shut; I can't hear the bang of course but I do hear Granddad putting his wine glass down on the table.

He calls himself an aesthete; I haven't the faintest idea what that means though. All I know is that he reads the great German poets like Goethe and Schiller, and philosophers, and he's got loads of records of them in all sorts of languages. The wine is to do with being an aesthete too.

The red liquid is still swaying sluggishly around the glass. I'd give anything to think of a change of subject, but I just slide around on the edge of my seat, nervous.

'Don't you want to know what it's like with boys?' asks Granddad, suddenly coming right up close to my face – he has to move onto the edge of his own seat but he's not nervous, he's perfectly calm and he puts his old hands on my knees.

They're like leather. I can feel the leather even through my jeans, his dry fingers, his thick blue veins. And I can smell the red wine on his breath, red wine and something sour. I think it's the smell of old age; at least I can't think of any other explanation.

I just shake my head again. The clock behind me ticks away. I can hear children yelling in the back yard. Everything else is silent.

'You know you're my favourite granddaughter,' Granddad says to my mouth. 'I don't want the boys to hurt you.'

I try not to breathe. My legs are tingling as if I had to jump up and run away. I nod because I can't think of anything better to do, and stare at his hands clutching my knees.

5

Beate Teresa Hanika

Then he strokes my head, gathering up my hair at the back of my neck; it's light-brown with ringlets at the end.

'You're so beautiful,' he says. 'You look so like your gran.'

I don't know why I don't move.

Even when he kisses me, fast and hard on the lips, I hold quite still.

I feel his lips knocking against mine as if they were made of stone, and he knocks the glass at the same time. The wine runs over the table and drips onto the floor. The doorbell rings at that very moment.

It's Anne and Dad.

Anne's seventeen. She has long blonde hair and a huge amount of freckles all over her pale face. She's doing her A-levels and she thinks she's better than everyone else. She sits in the front of the car on the way home. She always sits in the front. And she's always listening to her iPod. She closes her eyes as she listens, eyes with black eyeliner around them that I find scary, and nods her head along with the music. Normally, I nudge her from behind. I bore my pointed knees into the seat and really wind her up – my revenge for her never letting me sit in the front. But I don't feel like it today.

From the back seat, I watch my father driving. He has a bald head that looks polished in the sun, and a moustache; but I can only see one end of it from where I'm sitting in the back. Usually, we

6

don't say a word on the whole journey; it's only ten minutes anyway, we might as well go by bike. Then I look out of the window and imagine I have a horse on a rein that I have to break in. It runs along next to the car, and the grass verge next to the road is the racetrack. I spur my horse on – her name's Mary-Lou and she runs like the wind. It's a stupid game for a thirteen-year-old but I don't tell anyone, so it's all right.

I don't even feel like playing it today.

I slide into the gap between the two front seats, even though Dad hates it when I do that.

'Granddad kissed me today,' I say, or I hear myself saying.

'I don't want him to kiss me again.'

Dad doesn't say anything at all.

For a moment I think he doesn't hear me.

Then I feel him looking at me in the rear-view mirror. Just for a moment, then he concentrates on the road again.

I fall back onto the seat and bore my knees into my sister's back.

'Stop it, you little beast,' she growls without even taking her earphones out, and pinches my leg as hard as she can.

I feel like crying.

After dinner I jump on my bike and disappear.

My mother doesn't like it when I go out on my own on my bike in the evening, because so many things might happen. She's always scared for me, at least that's what she says, but I've started to suspect she's just bored when I'm not at home. She says girls shouldn't ride around on their own. So I lie to her and tell her my best friend Lizzy's coming with me, even though I know full well that Lizzy left for her skiing trip this afternoon.

I lie quite often because my mother's so difficult.

I lie to reassure her, and sometimes I don't tell her things so she doesn't get upset. When she gets upset she gets a migraine, and that means we have to creep around the darkened house, taking care not to make a sound.

So today I am going for a bike ride with Lizzy.

She still gives me a punishing look, hurt because I'm not staying at home.

'You'd better be back by seven-thirty!' she shouts after me.

I pretend I didn't hear anything and carry on pedalling.

I like being on my own.

I'll go to the villa.

It's an old vacant house where we used to play. Now we're too old – for playing. I'm the only person who still goes to the villa, and I go there a lot. It's a little way away from the last road in the new estate, surrounded by apple and pear trees; you have to crawl through a gap in the fence and then wade through waist-high grass.

I ride as fast as I can until I get a stitch. The sun is

already low in the sky, casting a slanted shadow ahead of me. My legs are much too long for the bike; I'm as thin as a rake and I'll probably never get breasts.

The road through the new estate runs uphill. I push right down on the pedals; my bike's really ancient, it used to belong to my brother. The gears are broken and by the time I get to the top my lungs are burning. This is where the track begins and I have time to catch my breath. The villa crouches behind the trees like an old, sleeping animal. I glide down the last curves of the path.

I crawl through the gap in the fence and stomp through the grass, dried up from the winter.

Last year Lizzy and I defended the villa against the boys from the new estate. I even got in a fight with one of them. He was the biggest of them all, at least two years older than us.

I was so scared of him! We'd barricaded the door and leaned our shoulders against it.

'They'll never get it open,' Lizzy said, brushing her dark hair out of her eyes.

'Never!'

He just kicked it in. Then everything happened really quickly. He wanted to push us back so the other boys could come in after him. They shoved their way through the hole, and he, the leader, pushed me. I got angry – no, I was already angry before that. All of a sudden I drew back my arm and whacked him in the face with my fist, like my brother had always shown me.

'Malvina,' he always says, 'girls never punch properly, they punch with the soft side of their fists,' then he grabs my hand and clenches my fist. 'Look, like this' – he says and hits the bottom of my fist against his chest – 'it doesn't hurt at all. You have to punch with your knuckles, and your wrist has to be straight and firm so you don't bend your hand back…'

And that's how I punched him.

And the boy held his hand in front of his face – his nose was bleeding like mad, it was pulsing and spraying blood all over everything, the floor, my T-shirt, my bare arms. The boys scrambled head over heels back outside through the hole.

Since then the door of the villa's been kicked in and our fight's been over.

They never came back, all summer long.

We were bored for the rest of the summer.

This is the first time I've been here this year.

It's an unwritten law that we leave the villa in peace over the winter. I don't even come near the estate in winter.

Everything is just how we left it. The broken door is hanging from its hinges. With a little goodwill you can spot the bloodstains on the floorboards. I don't like the downstairs rooms much. There must have been a fire here at some point. The walls are black, there's a burnt sofa in the corner, and old magazines are scattered across the floor. Women's magazines from 1990 and even porn mags – nothing hard core, just naked women, so shredded and torn you can't make much out anyway.

The rooms on the first floor are still all right. There's even an old wood-burning stove where you can light a fire, and living-room furniture with framed photos that we love looking at in awe.

One of the photos is of a man in uniform. He looks really strict. We call him Evil Frederick.

'Whooo, Evil Frederick's haunting this place,' Lizzy says every time we're in this room, giving us cold shivers down our backs.

I wouldn't want to come across Evil Frederick...

The attic room is my kingdom.

I climb up the wooden staircase. The pigeons spot me far too late and flutter through the holes between the beams in shock. Their feathers cover the floor like soft down.

'Shhh...shhh...' I say, 'no need to be scared of me, you know me...'

But they still shy away from me, beating their wings and stepping nervously to and fro on the beams.

The whole room is empty apart from a huge mattress with cushions and covers that I dragged up here with my own hands, under the part of the roof that doesn't leak. In the beams above it hangs a floor-length pink curtain, like over a four-poster bed. Lizzy got hold of that. She's got loads of cheesy stuff at home but it looks really good here.

Every time I come back here I'm scared it'll all be gone or trashed.

I fall backwards onto the cushions with my eyes closed; they smell of hay and fieldmice, of spring and old feathers.

Winter is over.

On the ridge of the roof perches a blackbird, singing of the evening, how the day's almost over and how the world will grow dangerous then. I wish I could go to sleep, for ever and ever, stay here between these cushions and listen to the blackbirds and the pigeons, here where nobody can find me.

I open my eyes as a shadow crosses my face.

It's the boy.

We stare each other in the face.

Suddenly, I'm scared and try to stare back as meanly as I can.

'What do you want here?' I ask him with a voice that sounds firm and brave.

The boy just shrugs. He's crouching in front of me. I can see that his nose is slightly out of joint, and I'm afraid that's my fault and now he wants to settle the matter with me, now the two of us are alone here and no one can hear me.

He must be much stronger than me; he's not taller but he's got broader since last time I saw him. He's got proper muscles on his arms, I can tell through his sweatshirt.

I secretly clench my fists, just in case.

Then he grins.

'I know who you are,' he says.

For a moment my heart skips a beat. I think he's going to say:

You're the girl who broke my nose.

'I've got your father for biology. He's a real bastard.'

He doesn't look at me as he says it, and I'm glad because I flinch as if this time it was him hitting me in the face.

I don't know what to say. I ought to defend my father but I can't think of anything. And anyway I know the kids in his classes don't like him. He's very strict; not just at school, at home too.

He's the only teacher at the school by the estate who gives detentions; I think even the other teachers don't like him much.

The boy gets up and leans against the flimsy old rafters.

He's on the side towards the estate. He casually fishes a crumpled pack of cigarettes out of his pocket.

'Want one?' he asks, not waiting for an answer but lighting one up for himself. The smoke fills the room like fog, annoying me because it bothers my pigeons. They get all nervous and start cooing, retreating as far back from him as possible.

I get up.

It doesn't feel particularly good sitting below him. I don't trust him – after all it was me who humiliated him in front of all the others last year, and he's got my father at school.

I don't know which is worse.

'Is it true your father used to be a boxer?'

I look at him, surprised. We're standing next to one another and his face reflects the sunset, I notice he's quite good-looking. I can't tell what colour his eyes are but he has long dark eyelashes, almost like a girl.

I quickly look away again, in the same direction as him, towards the estate.

'Yes, he was,' I say, 'but that's a long time ago.'

And he wasn't a professional either. But I don't say that, it doesn't make any difference.

'He still does his training,' I add. 'He's got a punchbag in the cellar. He does it every day.'

The boy nods as if he'd thought so all along.

'He nearly hit a boy in my class once. Benny, his name was, he was older than us because he had to repeat a year twice, and he thought he was really clever. He threw a firecracker at the board in the middle of a lesson...*Whoosh*...! Your father knew just who it was. He walked up to him, all calm and we thought he was going to hit him in the face.'

There's an awkward silence.

'If you hit back within three seconds it's a reflex, that's OK. I'd do it,' he says, and draws his arm back as if he is going to take a swing at someone.

The pigeons fly up in fright. They've had enough for today; they circle once around the villa, flutter wildly and then fly over to the estate.

Suddenly I'm scared he'll ask me if my father's like that at home.

I wish I could say he's the nicest man in the world. But I don't want to lie to him.

He doesn't ask. He flicks the butt of his cigarette across the roof; it rolls down into the guttering, still smoking for a few seconds, then goes out.

'Do you live over there?' I ask, even though I already know the answer.

'Mmm,' says the boy, 'in Sunny Park.'

Very scornful, he is.

'It's getting even bigger now, they're tearing this wreck down soon to build a supermarket...'

He gives me a quick glance from the side.

Now I really feel sick, as if someone is pressing down on my throat, and I can feel the tears behind my eyes, that have been just waiting for an opportunity all day.

They couldn't have chosen a worse one.

'I've got to go,' I say, fighting to stay calm, then I turn round and race down the staircase.

'Hey,' he shouts after me, 'what's your name?'

But I'm already running out of the villa, and about time too because the tears are splashing out of my eyes now. Tears of anger that hardly come up through my throat.

I could shout and scream over all this injustice. The boy stays up there until I disappear into the estate.

That bloody estate!

Saturday

Back when Lizzy and I discovered the villa, the boys from the estate didn't even exist. Well, they did exist – they just lived somewhere else. Where the estate is now, there were just fields and meadows and a little pond full of duckweed. We swam in it in summer; there was a jetty for running up and jumping into the water. We held hands and tried to jump as far as we could. Learning to fly, we called it.

Then they filled in the pond because it took up too much space, and now there are two semi-detached houses on top of it and the people in the houses don't even know Lizzy and I used to swim there.

Once the pond was gone we went to the villa. We painted black skull and crossbones on white bed-sheets and hung them up in the windows, as a sign that the villa belonged to us. Just us, and Lizzy said it didn't matter that pirate flags are actually the other way round, white on black. It's the thought that counts.

'When needs must, you just have to improvise,' she said.

The boys laughed at us of course when they saw the flags. They cycled round and round the villa, again and again, and whispered to each other so we couldn't hear what they were planning next. Then they threw stones through the empty windows and shouted up at us, *Hey, you scaredy cats*, and Lizzy and I sat in Evil Frederick's living room and didn't dare to breathe.

'God, Lizzy,' I said, 'they'll make mincemeat out of us if they catch us.'

The stones landed nearby, not big ones but big enough to hurt if you happened to get hit. One of them smashed the picture of Evil Frederick, the one where he's wearing his uniform and looks really fierce; it made such a loud crash that they stopped throwing, and Lizzy whispered:

'One more stone and they'll see what happens when they mess with us.'

If you asked her, it was all the boys' fault that the pond was gone. It had to be someone's fault, and the boys were the first people we could lay our hands on. One of them even lived in one of those houses, a short fat boy who was always chewing gum and blowing huge apple-green bubbles. We'd make them pay for living there.

Then came the next stone. It hit Lizzy on the shoulder and we jumped up and started throwing back. We threw everything we could get our hands on, and when Lizzy chucked an old pewter jug out of the window we heard them swearing and jumping onto their bikes. We peered round the sides of our flags to make sure they were really going.

The short fat boy stuck his bubble gum on the saddle of my bike as revenge – a huge green lump. You can still make out traces of it now. We saw him taking it out of his mouth, and I thought, thank God he's not sticking bogies on it.

'They wouldn't dare,' Lizzy said.

On Saturday, Granddad has a fall.

He wanted to go downstairs to the bins in the back yard, and then he had a fall, he says. Because the neighbour on his floor, Mrs Bitschek, left her baby's buggy in the corridor again. Mrs Bitschek has always been a thorn in Granddad's side. She comes from Poland and has five little children who are always making a racket and jumping around on the stairs, and when Granddad wants to talk to her and tell her to keep her children quiet, she just shakes her head and says: 'No understand!' And Granddad thinks she understands him just fine, she just doesn't want to.

'That's the problem with these people, they just don't want to understand,' he says.

He grazed his hands in the fall and hurt his knee. His knee hurts day in day out anyway, and now he can't move it at all, he has to put an ice pack on it and keep still or the pain goes right through him from his big toe to the tips of his hair.

'It's not my fault he fell over,' I say.

My mother is lying down in her darkened bedroom – and a good thing too, that way I can't see her long-suffering expression. Next to her bed are her medicine and a glass of water, all just vague shapes in the fug. She grips my hand tightly because she knows how uncomfortable it makes me feel when she's like this. I usually go round to Lizzy's when she gets this way. I take my bike and leave a note on the kitchen table. It quite often makes her angry when she finds my notes, because I'm not looking after her. No one has to look after Lizzy's mother, she never has a migraine. And you're always allowed to be noisy at Lizzy's, you can listen to music as loud as you want and whenever you want, you can shout and scream all day long. Sometimes when we turn the music up too loud and jump around in her room, the neighbour downstairs knocks on the ceiling. Then we stop and Lizzy's mother comes in her room and puts her finger on her lips. 'Time out,' she says then, and Lizzy and I are absolutely silent until we burst out laughing.

That's what it's like at Lizzy's.

'Malvina,' says my mother, 'please.'

She smells of Tiger Balm because she dabs it on her temples. She thinks that makes her headache better. If you ask me it just makes you feel really sick. That smell has followed me all through my childhood – I can't remember her ever smelling any different.

I know exactly what she wants from me. She wants me to look after Granddad, she wants to pass the buck to me because she knows full well that Granddad always picks on her when she goes round. He says she's always looked so weedy and she'll never get a job if she carries on like this, and then he says, 'How old is Malvina now anyway, thirteen? Pretty long time for maternity leave.'

Granddad can be really mean.

'Why can't Mrs Bitschek take him something to eat? It was her buggy,' I say.

My mother gives a little sigh. She knows as well as I do that Granddad probably didn't have a fall. He makes things up when he's lonely, and since Gran's been gone he's often lonely.

'I'm not going on my own,' I say. 'I never go there on my own.'

She sighs again and presses my hand.

'You were there on your own yesterday,' she says. 'You don't have to stay long.'

'You've only got a headache because you don't want to go,' I snap at her.

A tiny shudder goes through her body, and I pull my hand away.

'The food's in the kitchen,' she says.

And that's that for her on the subject.

The whole house is dark. Anne's on the phone in her

room; I can hear her muffled voice through the door as I fetch the basket and the keys to my bike lock from the kitchen.

'You could do something for once!' I shout outside her room. Extra loudly, so my mother shudders and her headache gets even worse. 'Bugger off!' Anne shouts back.

I hang the basket on my handlebars and cycle off; it's not that easy because the basket sways to and fro and I have to be really careful not to lose my balance. I'm not actually allowed to hang anything on the handlebars because it's much too dangerous, but I don't care today. I have to go right across town down a steep slope called Gallows Hill. I feel the wind on my face and let my bike coast, thinking about whether to close my eyes like Lizzy does now and then. She does it to wind me up.

'I'm blind,' she yells, 'tell me when we get to the traffic lights...'

There are traffic lights at the very bottom of the hill. You have to brake really hard when you're going fast. I always pretend I'm not scared for her, but of course I am scared, I can't help it – she's my best friend, isn't she?

'Don't ever do that again,' I always say when we end up eye to eye at the crossroads, and Lizzy just shrugs and grins at me.

'Slowcoach!'

I shut my eyes for a tiny moment – not quite

closed, I can see the blurred traffic lights coming closer through the slits like green fairy lights, houses rush past me left and right, and someone shouts something, someone standing waving between the cars at the edge of the road, all I see of course is a blurry dab of blue, nothing else, but I hear what he calls out.

'Hey, Little Red Riding Hood!' he shouts, and I open my eyes again and there he is right next to me, the boy from the estate.

We brake at the traffic lights, which of course stupidly enough change to red at that very moment, and the boy grabs my arm.

'Are you crazy?' he says, breathless.

He doesn't know I didn't have my eyes closed properly, and I act like it was perfectly normal, nothing special, something I do every day.

I shrug and give him a superior grin. Just like Lizzy.

'Racing down the hill like Road Runner, with your eyes closed – I can't believe it!'

'I didn't ask your opinion,' I spit back at him and shake off his arm so I can straighten up my basket.

That's all I need. It's bad enough what he said about the villa, as if it was just what he wanted that the estate is getting bigger and bigger, that they're pulling down the villa, now it's all settled that it belongs to Lizzy and me and not them. No wonder he doesn't like it. I'd be angry too if I was him.

'You can't trust those boys,' Lizzy had said last summer. 'Don't you ever get mixed up with one of them.'

The lights switch to green and I pedal off.

'Where are you off to?' he says, cycling so close behind me that his front tyre nearly touches my back tyre. Boys always do that, I don't know why. It's happened to me a hundred times on the way to school. It usually ends up with me falling off – school-bag and all – or getting off my bike so I don't fall. At any rate it is embarrassing in front of everyone. They all laugh and shout after me that I need stabilisers.

'I didn't know that was any of your business,' I say, not turning round.

He whistles through his teeth, coming even closer until our tyres make a grinding sound and my bike starts swaying dangerously.

'Look at Little Miss Moody,' he says.

I turn off onto a side street; it's actually a detour but I don't want him to follow me all the way to Granddad's house. If I just ignore him he might leave me alone. There are hardly any cars here and the boy catches up and comes alongside me.

'Why did you just run away yesterday?' he asks.

He has no intention of leaving me alone; he looks like he's got all the time in the world, as if all his friends had gone skiing or caught the flu at the same time, as if he was really really bored and really really happy to have caught me at the traffic lights.

'I had to go home,' I say.

I know full well that's a stupid answer. No one just ups and runs away just because they have to go home, but I can't think of anything else, and you can't just say you were crying all the way home because of some old falling-down villa, or at least I don't want to say that to him. And anyway I quite often just up and run away.

'Aha,' he says, peering over at my basket piled high with Tupperware boxes and a bottle of wine.

We cycle around Granddad's block in a big circle. After the third time, I finally turn onto the right street and then into the dingy little backyard the tenants share, with bleached washing always hanging on the line and rubbish overflowing out of the bins.

At the other end of the yard under the horse chestnut trees, Mrs Bitschek is sitting on a bench joggling her buggy, the baby screaming its head off. The baby's always screaming when I see it. Mrs Bitschek says it's because of the electric smog, because there's a transformer station right next to the building, you can even hear it humming if you listen carefully. But Granddad says that's rubbish, the baby screams because everyone from over there, the Poles, they all scream like that, it's in their nature. And Mrs Bitschek says, 'Electro no good.'

'You visit Granddad again?' she yells over at us, still joggling away.

I nod, a bit annoyed because now the boy knows what I'm doing here. We get off our bikes, I fumble around with my combination lock for ages on purpose so I don't have to look at him and hope he'll just disappear, but when I look up again, my face bright red, he's still there and grinning at me.

'Didn't I say Little Red Riding Hood?' he says and folds his arms as if he had nothing better to do than stand around and watch me.

Mrs Bitschek pushes the buggy slowly across the yard towards us. She has blonde permed hair with dark roots and a friendly round face with a double chin.

'Hello,' she says. 'Your boyfriend?'

The boy grins.

'Right,' he says, and I'm so angry I could sink into the ground, but Mrs Bitschek doesn't notice. She looks from one to the other of us, really thrilled.

'How lovely,' she says. 'Young love!'

The back door is open and I walk up the stairs, the basket banging against my knee. Granddad's key is in the lock so I don't have to ring the bell. I lean my red-hot face against the wood of the door. Young love! As if. If only she knew! I can hear her from here, telling the boy I'm such a nice girl, how I look after my granddad, how pretty I've got this last year, all in her broken English. She even tells him my gran died last year and what of: cancer. The boy doesn't say anything. He doesn't even know my name.

I turn the key in the lock and the door jerks open. It's hot and muggy in the flat. Much too hot.

Granddad always turns all the radiators right up so he doesn't get cold.

He's lying on the sofa in the living room, wrapped in a brown checked blanket.

'My little Malvina,' he says, 'here you are at last.'

I put the basket down on the table, next to a bottle of wine, a glass and a plate full of crumbs. He's already eaten.

'Your hands aren't grazed,' I say.

They're resting on the checked blanket, wrinkled and absolutely untouched, and he pretends not to have heard me.

He was lying again, of course. He pats the space next to him as a sign for me to sit down with him.

'You shouldn't talk to Mrs Bitschek,' he says, so I know he's seen me from the window. 'You mustn't have anything to do with them, they don't belong here.'

I sit down on the floor next to the couch and hug my arms around my knees. Mum says we mustn't contradict Granddad, otherwise he'll get upset and angry, and when he gets really angry he doesn't know what he's doing. Then he forgets he's actually an aesthete.

She says it's better to let him talk and just think your own thoughts. Lizzy says you always have to say what you think, right away, but I don't usually dare. Otherwise I'd say right now that I really like Mrs Bitschek, even though her baby's always crying and the other kids run around in the corridor.

'Who was that boy?' he asks, giving me a sharp look.

I dig my fingernails into my ankles and shrug.

'Don't know,' I say.

Granddad sits up. I hate it when he looks at me like that, as if I've done something wrong.

'You're lying,' he says. 'I heard every word he said. He said he's your boyfriend. Don't you lie to me.'

And then he says how disappointed he is in me, and that I can trust him, that he won't tell anyone my little secret, it's our secret now, and he takes no notice of me saying over and over that I don't know the boy.

I don't even know his name. We never talked to the boys last summer. We gave them our own names, secret names like Hubba Bubba for the boy with the bubble gum, and we called one of them Puddle because he was so pale and always looked a bit ill, and then there was one who never pulled a face, who always just stared straight ahead, and he was called Poker Face. And then the boy. We just called him Screwy.

Lizzy called him that because she thought he definitely had a screw loose.

'That Screwy's not quite right in the head,' she used to say. 'We'll have to really watch out for him.'

I thought all the others were just as bad, but for Lizzy this one boy was way worse than the others.

'Did you see his eyes?' she asked me once, and I said no. Back then I'd never seen him close up, but

Lizzy said in a sinister voice: 'But I have, I've seen them...'

I can't tell Granddad that, of course; that the boy's name is Screwy.

So I say I have to go now because of Mum's migraine, but Granddad doesn't believe a word, he thinks I want to go back to the boy. That's crystal clear to him.

He pulls me up next to him onto the sofa. It's so old and saggy the springs squeak under our weight, I can even feel them poking into my bottom.

I'm certain he didn't fall down the stairs, there's nothing wrong with him. He doesn't look like he's in any pain.

'I don't like it at all,' he says, 'that that lad's more important to you. You know I need you at the moment, now I'm ill and your gran's not here any more.'

He makes a sad face as if he felt like crying because I don't like him any more. He's only acting – his face looks like a mask, as if he'd pulled on a sad clown's mask that he could take off again with a flick of his wrist.

'You do love me, don't you?' he says and runs his fingertips across my forehead, my nose, my mouth, down to my throat and up to the neck of my T-shirt. They hover there, holding still for a moment as if they were waiting for an answer.

I nod and feel awful because I don't love him, not at all, I'm scared of him, I just didn't know it before.

But now I know it full well, I know he scares me when he looks at me like this.

'Then give me a little kiss before you go,' he says, hugging his arms around me really tightly. I can feel his bony chest, his hands on my back stroking my shoulder blades, and I hear my heart beating loud in my head, in my ears and my neck, as if it wanted to leap out of my body and run away.

'I can't,' I say, because you always have to say what you think.

Granddad laughs then and kisses me again, like yesterday, and I hold my breath and press my lips together until I think I'm going to faint any minute, any minute now I won't be able to hold my breath any longer and I'll die.

'You'll be back tomorrow,' he says.

Sunday

'Let's swear that we'll never have anything to do with the boys from the estate,' said Lizzy last summer, after we'd scraped the green bubble gum off my saddle together – we did it together because we both thought it was really disgusting, so it was only fair, and Lizzy scraped a bit more off than me because I was the one who'd have to put my bum on the saddle for the rest of my life. The dust the boys had whirled up with their bikes was still hanging in the air, and all around us lay the stuff out of Evil Frederick's living room.

'Yuck,' I said, wiping my fingers on my jeans. There was nothing I'd rather have done than swear that I'd never have anything to do with the boys from the estate. I wouldn't anyway, I thought. Who'd want to hang out with someone who throws stones and sticks bubble gum on other people's bike saddles?

Then we went back into the villa because Lizzy decided we ought to seal our oath with blood – without blood it was only messing around, nothing serious, so we looked around the villa for a suitable tool for our solemn deed.

'We need a knife,' said Lizzy, and even the word 'knife' made me feel sick – I can't stand the sight of blood, even the tiniest drop makes me feel uncomfortable, but I knew nothing on earth would put Lizzy off her plan. That's just the way Lizzy is; she does exactly what she says, never mind what happens.

I tried not to find a knife, which was pointless of course, I knew it from the start. And then Lizzy did find one in one of the burnt-out rooms, one with a blade covered in soot – that was just what we needed, Lizzy said.

We took the knife up to the attic, up to the pigeons, and Lizzy leaped around under the beams, shaking the knife about so the pigeons got a good fright.

'This is the ceremonial blood-sisters' dance!' she cried, and then she plonked herself down on the mattress, our four-poster bed. We sat opposite each other, our legs crossed, Lizzy pretty out of breath and me scared because of the knife. She put it down between the two of us with the blackened blade pointing upwards.

'Don't do that,' I told her, 'you'll cut a friendship.' That's what my gran always said when anyone accidentally left a knife with the blade upwards.

'Of course, that's just why I'm doing it,' Lizzy said. 'Three guesses which friendship I want to cut…'

We held hands above the knife, and I objected that we hadn't even been friends with the boys, and Lizzy told me not to split hairs and to shut my mouth and only open it to repeat the words of our oath after her.

The pigeons fluttered back to their beams above us, feathers floated down to the mattress, and Lizzy lowered her voice to a mysterious whisper.

'I, Lizzy, solemnly swear by my blood to take eternal revenge and be the eternal enemy of the boys from the estate.'

She squeezed my hands and looked deep into my eyes; she has hazel eyes with golden flecks.

'I, Malvina,' I whispered, 'solemnly swear by my blood to take eternal revenge and be the eternal enemy of the boys from the estate…'

'…and I swear,' I added, 'to stick a whole packet of apple-flavour Hubba Bubba on every one of their saddles.'

We grinned at each other, and Lizzy took the knife. She pressed the blade against the tip of her forefinger and a tiny drop of blood pearled out, which she dripped onto a gold-rimmed saucer. That was where we wanted to mix our blood.

'Quick,' she said, 'your turn.'

I felt very brave, back then, as I took the knife from her with a dignified expression and cut into my finger. It didn't hurt at all, the blood dripped onto Lizzy's blood and Lizzy said, 'Blood sisters for ever,' and I said: 'Oh dear, I feel sick,' and then I blacked out.

Every Sunday, I wait for my brother Paul to come home.

As long as it's not raining I sit on the wall of our front garden, no matter how cold it is, so I can see him coming as soon as his car turns into our road. Sometimes I sit there for ages, especially when Mum's feeling ill again and the house is dark. Dad's in a bad mood because Mum's ill and because he has to mark homework, and Anne's on the phone to her thousands of friends. Then I could sit on the wall and watch the road for hours.

There's nothing better than when Paul comes home from uni. Before we go inside he sits down on the wall with me.

'What's up?' he says, and then I tell him what was up all week. It all comes flooding out, everything I can't tell Mum because it would upset her too much, about school and what Lizzy and I have been up to. I talk and talk for at least ten minutes, and he just listens until I run out of steam, and then he says:

'We'll sort it all out.'

Lizzy really envies me Paul. She hasn't got any brothers or sisters and she'd give anything to have a big brother like him. When we were little we made a deal to share him. I was supposed to get half of her guinea-pig Monty in exchange. But then Monty died, and really you just have to have a brother of your

33

own; a guinea-pig just can't match up, even though Monty was really cute. Sharing a brother just doesn't work. There's nothing you can do. And I wouldn't want the three of us to sit on the wall together, even though Lizzy's my very best friend.

I've been sitting on the garden wall for exactly forty-three minutes now.

Mum's still got a migraine. The doctor came round yesterday and gave her an injection, then she always sleeps through to the next morning and then it starts up all over again. This morning I woke up to the sound of Mum puking. These days are the worst, the days when she starts vomiting in the morning. I make sure I'm out of the house on days like these.

If a silver car comes past and then two black ones, I tell myself, the next one will be Paul.

If I really concentrate it works. Not always of course, but sometimes. But today neither a silver car nor a black one drives past. It's as if our street were dead, as if the whole world had a migraine. There's only me sitting out here and holding my face and my bare arms out to the sun, very pale with light-brown freckles.

At long last I hear the sound of an engine; it's Paul, I know that even before I see the car. When he turns the corner I wave like crazy. Behind the windscreen, even though the glass is reflecting the sun, I can make out his blond mop of hair and his sunglasses; he wears them because they look cool and the girls are into cool guys. He beeps back at me – it sounds completely unreal, it's so quiet here.

I hop down from the wall because I can't wait to talk to him, while Paul parks his car alongside the pavement.

'Hey!' he says and whirls me around until I get dizzy. 'How's my little sister?'

He puts me down on the bonnet.

'You need to eat more,' he says and looks me up and down. 'You're much too thin.'

He's said that nearly every time since I started growing.

I wanted to tell him about Granddad, about the kissing and about the boy, but now I can't get my mouth open and I've got a nasty lump in my throat, as if I'd swallowed the green ball of bubble gum from last summer and one bit was stuck half-way down my throat and the other half was further down.

Every time I think of Granddad I feel ashamed; it's a really nasty feeling, as if I'd done something wrong. As if the kiss ought to embarrass me.

Every time I think of it my stomach starts to rotate, like on a carousel but worse. So I try to think about it as little as possible, not about Granddad and not about how I have to visit him again. I'm quite good at it. I just think really quickly about Lizzy or the boy, and this morning I mostly thought about Paul and wished really hard that he'd understand me and say I don't have to go to Granddad's again, never again, or at least not on my own.

Paul rocks the car up and down.

We used to play that quite a lot in our old Ford. Paul sat on the bonnet and made the car rock to and fro, and Anne and I pretended we were on a sinking ship.

Titanic, the game was called, and when I closed my eyes I could see the sea, the towering waves, sea monsters and sharks, and I could feel what it's like to drown, I could feel it quite clearly. How the water swallows you up and sucks you deeper and deeper until it's dark all around you, dark and cold, and you know you're going to die. I don't think Anne thought about drowning for a single second.

We squealed and squealed until we were hoarse, we squealed until Paul didn't want to rock us any more.

'About Granddad...' says Paul. 'You're going to have to apologise to him.'

I flinch. Dad's told him. So that's the way it is. Dad's told Paul the thing about Granddad. They've been talking about me behind my back, that's so cruel, and they think I should apologise for telling tales on him.

Paul stops rocking and puts his arm around my shoulders, and my shoulders suddenly feel terribly cold.

'Granddad doesn't mean it like that. You know how much he likes you, don't you? He loves you the best out of all of us.'

I don't answer and he squeezes my shoulders even harder, really firmly, as if he understood me. But inside I know he doesn't have the faintest idea.

He just doesn't have the faintest idea.

Not about me and not about Granddad.

He wasn't there, he didn't see Granddad, and he hasn't heard how Granddad talks to me. How can I explain it all?

What I ought to say now is how sad I find it that nobody has the faintest idea about me, but I've still got that lump in my throat. I try to swallow it, but the lump stays firmly stuck there until I feel like I'm going to suffocate on it. Paul's arm around my shoulders makes the whole thing even worse. If his arm wasn't there I could jump down from the bonnet and act like I think the same way. I'd swallow the lump and laugh.

Granddad loves me best of all.

I'd say:

'Right, Granddad loves me best of all, I know that.'

I can feel how easy it would be to say those words, how I'd wipe my thoughts away with them, delete them from my mind so that everything's all right again.

Can you get Tippex for thoughts? And for feelings? Someone ought to invent it.

But his arm is holding me tight, and I know there's something wrong here.

If you love someone like Granddad does me there's something wrong, I'm sure.

I stare at the tips of my shoes, at the asphalt, at my freckled arms, so that I don't cry. Behind us someone pulls up the shutters with a jerk, probably Dad.

He says Mum has to pull herself together, you can't be ill all the time, so he opens the windows and bosses her out of bed and into the bathroom and waits until she's dressed. Not just her dressing gown; properly dressed.

'All this lying around won't do your headache any good,' he says, and then Mum suffers in silence to punish him and carries her pot of Tiger Balm around the house with her so that everyone can see what she has to put up with, so that everyone can see how ill she is.

Dad slams the windows. 'At least when your son comes home,' I hear him say. I can't make out what Mum answers but it sounds very tearful.

'He kissed me,' I say quietly.

Paul laughs.

'But I kiss you too,' he says.

But he kisses me quickly. On the cheek, on my ear or on my hair. Not like Granddad; he does it the proper way.

Like you kiss someone you really love.

'You see,' he says, 'it's as simple as that.'

Then he jumps down from the bonnet as if he had to go inside very quickly, as if he was suddenly in a big rush. There's a dent in the metal where he was sitting. A print of his behind. He gives me a wonky grin, as if he wasn't quite sure himself, and I grin back.

It's as simple as that.

I lock myself in the bathroom.

I don't want any lunch, I don't want to talk to Paul any more, all I want is to be on my own. Dad hammers on the door and shouts, 'What are you doing in there?'

'Having a bath,' I say, 'I'm in the bathtub.'

That's not true, of course, and Dad shouts that he lives in a madhouse where people get in the bathtub in the middle of the afternoon and other people lie in bed all day long. 'It's impossible round here,' he shouts. 'You're not doing this to me!' Have I thought about the water bill, he's the one who has to pay it, all these baths every day, and if I carry on like this he'll cement the bathtub up. 'Cement it up!' he shouts.

I press my hands against my ears until I can't hear anything except a slight drumming, but it's not my father outside the door, it's my heart. Crouched down, I squat in the bathtub and wait until I'm sure he's gone, sure I'm alone.

An hour ago he pressed a couple of notes into my hand, from Granddad, so I'll come back and bring him his lunch. Every day until he's better, and the money's to make up for it. For the bike ride, for the time I spend with him during the holidays.

'Granddad's very grateful to you,' he said, giving my head a quick stroke.

He never does that.

Mum says that's just the way Dad is. He's not very good at showing his feelings, she says, but that doesn't mean he doesn't love us. He shows it in other ways, ways you don't always understand right away. He earns money so we can afford the house and two holidays a year. She can't usually think of much else apart from that. Sometimes she says he only tells me off because he means well, because he wants me to have a good life later on, and if I don't do well at school he worries I won't get a decent job. That's why he shouts and rants when I don't get good marks. That means he's going crazy out of worry.

Having feelings and showing feelings are two different things.

But I still can't get the thought out of my head that something's wrong about Dad's feelings.

'I'm not going,' I said and locked myself in the bathroom.

I'm still holding the money in my hand, a sweaty bundle of paper. I can hear a murmur of voices from the kitchen. If I listened carefully with my ear to the bathroom door I'd hear what they're saying, but I know anyway. I don't need to get out of the bathtub for that.

Dad's saying how stubborn I am, that he doesn't know what to do with me any more.

'She just plays deaf,' he's saying, 'in one ear and out the other.'

And Paul's saying, 'It's her age.'

I chuck the bundle of paper at the toilet, only hitting the edge, and then I hear another sound from outside. That does make me sit up. Stupidly enough, the bathroom window is frosted glass so you can't see a thing no matter how hard you look; all you can make out is shapes and nothing else. But it's slightly open at the top and if you peer through the gap you can see out onto the street. You can see our garden gate, a bit of the wall, the path from the house to the road.

And on the road is the boy.

He's riding past. On his bike, so fast I don't recognise him right off; at first I think I'm mistaken, but then he comes back, slower this time.

Screwy.

I get such a shock I nearly fall back into the tub.

What's he doing here?

He turns a couple of circles outside our garden gate, so slowly he must be dragging his feet on the ground.

He's not going to ring the doorbell! Oh God, please don't let him ring the doorbell!

I slip away from the window. It'd be so embarrassing if he saw me here. And then I do peer out again.

He's pretty good-looking, I have to admit. I don't even want to think about what Lizzy would say to that. She'd say he looks like a mad person with a screw loose, and then she'd say I should put that idea out of my mind, whatever, just not think about it.

An oath's an oath. A blood sister's a blood sister. And she's right too.

He's tied his hair back in a little bunch, standing out from the back of his head like a thick brush of horsehair. He's wearing faded jeans with holes in the knees and the bum and a black T-shirt. Even though it's not particularly warm.

Boys don't seem to get cold that easily.

You can make out the shape of a cigarette packet in his pocket. I can only hope Mum doesn't catch sight of him. She'd think he's really rough. Even just the holes in his jeans. She thinks people shouldn't walk around like that. 'Clothes make the man,' she's always saying.

She usually says it to Lizzy, because Lizzy has holes in her jeans too and wears stripy tights underneath, and sometimes she doesn't have anything underneath, and that's the worst. Holes with nothing underneath. I know what she's got underneath, of course. G-strings – she even let me try a pair on last week before she went skiing. I said G-strings are really uncomfortable, and Lizzy said, 'Baby, you have no idea!' and then we laughed and put the knickers over our heads like hats.

Screwy props his bike up against our garden gate. Purposefully, he opens the gate and stamps along the path. He stops outside the bathroom window and looks up at me.

'I can see you standing behind the window,' he says, and I get such a shock I fall back into the bathtub, just like you're not supposed to do if you don't want to break your neck. Bathtubs can be incredibly dangerous if you're not careful and slip up.

'I said, I can see you standing behind the window,' he repeats, and throws a stone at the window frame. Probably just out of habit – he's always throwing stones. That's the trouble with bad habits, you can't help doing it over and over. Anne, for instance, bites her fingernails down to the quick, even though it hurts and her fingers sometimes look really awful; she still does it. Mum used to try and break the habit. She bought special bitter nail varnish so she'd stop, but it was no use, she carried on chewing her nails even with the varnish on them. I guess it's the same with Screwy and throwing stones.

'What d'you want?' I growl through the gap. 'Get out of here!'

There's a moment of silence and then he laughs quietly. He picks up a pebble and lets it slide from one hand to the other. He really is one sandwich short of a picnic!

'You didn't go to your granddad's today,' he says, 'I was waiting for you.'

Oh boy, is Lizzy going to be mad when she hears that. Waiting for me – pull the other one!

'Waiting in ambush, you mean,' I say. 'You lot are good at that, you don't need to tell me.'

We had enough tastes of that last summer. And now we're not even safe from them at home. It's about time Lizzy came back so we can clean up around here.

'Where are your mates?' I say, getting mean. 'I bet they're keeping a lookout behind the wall, aren't they?'

He looks around.

'Can't see anyone,' he says, grinning again.

I step from one foot to the other. I'm standing right in the puddle under the tap, in my socks. Dad's always having a fit about the tap because it drips, and that's a waste of energy, he says. That's why he insists we leave the plug in the bath so the water doesn't go to waste. Sometimes the bath is half-full of ice-cold water, and Mum says it might be better to call a plumber, and then Dad says she can do that with her money as soon as she goes back to work, and until then we'll just have to get used to the cold water.

My feet are soaking wet, anyway.

'Listen,' says the boy, 'are you coming to the villa tomorrow?'

He throws the stone up above his head and catches it blind behind his back. He's only doing it to impress me, of course. What a show-off. But I don't fall for that kind of thing; throwing some stupid pebble is hardly a party piece. He'll have to think of something else to impress me.

I don't answer. Instead I take a deliberately loud sniff so he knows right away what I think of that idea – not a lot.

'Well, think about it anyway,' he says, turning round and marching back down the path to the road, deliberately casual. He stops for a moment at the gate and throws the stone.

I can't see what he hits, all I can hear is a click, and I assume it's one of the bird houses my mother's put up in the garden. She can watch the birds for hours on end. If she hasn't got a migraine, that is.

Then he climbs back onto his bike in a very manly way, and I get to admire his bum again. He turns full circle and then cycles off. He doesn't look round.

I sit in the bath for the rest of the afternoon. I take off my socks and hang them over the edge of the tub to dry. I watch the tap dripping, watch the puddle getting bigger and bigger, and I watch the sky colouring darker. I can see that through the frosted glass.

Now and then my dad bashes at the door, and then Anne because she has to look in the mirror to see if her eyes still have black rims or her mascara's running. Lizzy and I have decided never to wear make-up. Because of Anne. We call her *barn owl* to wind her up, because she reminds us of a picture in the biology textbook we both have. *Brooding barn owl*, it says underneath, and Lizzy gave me a nudge and said it looked more like *Brooding Anne*, and then she crossed out the caption in pencil and wrote *Brooding Anne* next to it.

Twit-twoo, we say when she walks past. That makes her mad every time and she calls us ugly little toads.

'I don't care,' says Lizzy, 'I'd rather be an ugly toad than stupid.'

'Stupid cow!' Anne screams through the door, but I pretend to be deaf.

I stay in the bath when Paul goes too. He walks past the bathroom window; his laptop bag is probably slung over his shoulder. He doesn't stop.

See you next week, he could say, or keep your chin up. Just so I know he's thinking of me.

The car door slams.

I cry a bit because I know I'll never wait for him on the wall again, and I listen to the sound of his car engine getting quieter and quieter.

Monday

My gran died last May.

She'd got so thin and bald I hardly recognised her. It felt like she was disappearing more and more until there was nothing left of her.

'Malvina,' she said, 'I'm getting smaller and smaller, soon I'll be able to sleep in a shoe box. What do you say to that?'

I didn't say anything to that, because Gran was always tiny, just under one metre fifty, and because I knew she was right. Gran was always right about everything. She was a clever, gentle woman, she never shouted, and when Granddad shouted she used to smile.

'If you smile instead of losing your temper you're always the stronger one,' she used to say.

On the day of her funeral the sun smiled.

We stood around the grave and everyone cried,

especially my granddad and Anne and the old ladies from the church, the ones who always cry. My mother didn't cry, she stayed at home with a migraine. She can't stand funerals, all the people and the incense and the shaking hands at the end. She wishes she could just run away when everyone shakes her hand and says, 'My condolences.' She didn't even go to her own parents' funerals, my father had to go on his own with Paul and Anne. I was too young for funerals back then.

I'd never been to a funeral before.

Lizzy was standing next to me. We were wearing much-too-warm black clothes, and the sun shone down on us, and Lizzy said, 'Look, the sun's smiling because God's pleased your gran's going up to heaven at last.'

We were the only ones who didn't cry. We threw our flowers on the coffin and I couldn't believe my gran was really supposed to be lying down there – the coffin was big, much bigger than I'd imagined.

Much bigger than a shoe box.

She must look really lost in there, I thought.

After the funeral we went to the villa in our black clothes. We climbed around between the upstairs windows and I hoped the boys would come; I was in just the right mood for a fight, for screaming and shouting and throwing things out of the windows. The villa suddenly seemed so empty, as if a soul had moved out.

That's it, I thought, as if a soul had upped and left.

We kept a look-out for the boys for ages, giggling around, inventing silly games and sweating because it was hot and we didn't dare to take our black clothes off. Lizzy said, 'You're not allowed to on the day of a funeral, you have to walk around in black all day,' and I said, 'Maybe you're not allowed to laugh either.'

'Rubbish,' said Lizzy, 'why d'you think that?'

At some point we climbed up to the attic, and up there I couldn't stand the emptiness any more. I felt so absolutely miserable, I'd never felt that bad in all my life, and then I did start crying. I cried into the field-mice cushions, and Lizzy stroked my back. 'She's still here,' she said, stroking and stroking, and I got angry because I didn't believe her.

'She's not here at all,' I shouted. 'Don't lie to me!'

No answer. She just stopped stroking, pulled her hand away and gave me a very serious look. Lizzy had never lied to me before, I knew that for sure.

'Where is she then?' I screamed and ran wildly around the attic, from one side to the other, crying as I ran because I thought I couldn't bear the pain in my chest.

Lizzy didn't run round. She was sitting quite still on the mattress, and when I paused for a minute because I had a stitch from all the running and hiccups from the crying, I saw the sun shining through the roof beams above us in golden rays, with dust dancing and whirling in them, the air glowing and making haloes above our heads; at least that's what it looked like.

49

'Promise me,' I said, and Lizzy nodded and promised my gran wasn't just gone, that she'd always keep an eye on me and look after me, like a guardian angel.

'Promises have to be kept,' I whispered; I knew all about promises, and Lizzy said: 'Sure, I know that.'

Later we saw the boys from the estate coming along the track to the villa, but we didn't feel like a fight any more. We climbed out of one of the back windows and sneaked away. We watched them for a while from a distance, messing around in the villa, but it wasn't fun for long because they were on their own.

'They're bored,' said Lizzy.

'Next time they'll wish they were bored,' I said.

We're going round to Granddad's. Just Dad and me.

There's a cold silence in the car. I'm thinking furiously about what to do. Dad came into my room this morning; he closed the door behind him very emphatically and sat down at my desk. It looked funny because he never sits there, he hardly ever comes into my room. He looked at the posters above my bed for a while, posters of singers I like, and photos of Lizzy and me. He looked at them for ages, as if he'd never noticed I've got a friend before.

'So that's that Lizzy,' he said, and I didn't like the way he said *that Lizzy* and not just *Lizzy* or *your best friend Lizzy*.

I nodded and stared at the wall next to his head. There's a photo there of Lizzy and me, above my desk, that I really love. Lizzy's mother took it last summer, we're hugging and looking at the camera, and Lizzy's got a bruised eye. A real black eye; she looks really dangerous, like a pirate's daughter.

'I was just on the phone to Granddad,' Dad said. 'You've made him very sad. He can't understand why you don't want to visit him any more.'

That made me dizzy, right then and there, and I didn't know what to say so I bit my lip and didn't say anything and waited for him to go out again and leave me in peace.

'You listen to your feelings too much,' he said. 'You've got no sense, not one jot of sense.'

By that point I was so dizzy that Lizzy's face started turning circles on the photo and coming towards me; I had to close my eyes.

Everything's black, I thought. That's good.

Dad just carried on talking. He didn't care that I had my eyes closed, he didn't care; all he cared about was telling me about feelings, that you can't rely on them, that you can only count on your sense, and anyone with even five ounces of sense would see that your family always wants the best for you. And Granddad's family too.

Then at the end he said again: 'In one ear and out the other, that's always the way with you...'

And then my mother put her head round the door with her eyes screwed up as if it was really, really bright in my room and she was looking straight into the light, and Dad told her to mind her own business, her comments were all he needed now, and she left again without saying a word.

Granddad's left the key in the lock again.

'You shouldn't do that,' Dad tells him. 'Think of Mrs Bitschek.'

Granddad's lying on the sofa looking ill, the brown checked blanket pulled up to his chin.

'My Malvina,' he says.

I can't stand it here, not for one second. Mumbling an apology, I head for the toilet.

I tear open the window and take a deep breath. Warm spring air floods in. I lean right out; you can see the whole back yard from here. The horse chestnut trees are full of blossoms, like heavy white candles, and clouds are drifting above the sky, as fluffy as cotton wool balls. Directly below me is a little playground with demolished swings and a seesaw. I used to go down there a lot with Gran, every time I was here actually. There was a climbing frame that looked like a dragon. You could climb right through the body and a slide came out of its mouth, a really long slide. Gran used to pretend she was really scared for me when I clambered around inside it, and I used to pretend I was going to fall off any minute.

She put her hand on her heart and called out: 'Malvina, I can't stand it, it's all too much for me!'

I never did fall, of course; I always slid down the slide, straight into her arms.

The dragon slide's been gone for ages now. Someone ripped it out of the concrete a couple of years ago and tipped it over. Granddad said it was vandals; he meant the big boys from the block next door.

Mrs Bitschek walks across the yard and throws some bottles in the bin. She doesn't look up at me; the baby is perched on her hip, crying. Not as loudly as usual, the clinking of the bottles is much louder. I bet you can hear it three blocks away.

It's so loud I don't hear the front door closing. I only notice Dad's left when he steps out of the back door. He says hello to Mrs Bitschek with a brief nod and then he's gone, through the red and white barrier dividing the yard off from the road.

I stare at the barrier for a long time.

To be precise, I stare and stare until there's a knock at the door.

'Malvina,' says Granddad. He says it very softly. 'What are you doing in there for so long?'

When I open the door Granddad's still standing outside. He takes my hand and pulls me into the living room.

'You and I have something to talk about,' he says. 'Something very important.'

We sit down next to each other on the sofa, so close that our elbows and our knees touch.

'I sent your dad away,' he says.

He puts his arm around my shoulders as he says it. I can feel his arm shaking, I don't know why, it's shaking and it's so heavy that it pushes me down and down into the sofa.

'And do you know why I sent him away?' he asks, still really soft and quiet, like you might talk to a kitten or a bird caught in the hollow of your hand.

I turn my head away.

But Granddad takes hold of my chin and turns my head back so I can't help looking him in the eye.

He has one glass eye. His real eye is watery grey. The glass eye is clearer. I look into the glass eye.

'You know, those things you told your dad and Paul about us, they weren't nice. But your dad didn't believe you anyway. And do you know why?'

He stops for a moment and I wonder what it's like to have a glass eye, what it feels like in your eye socket, if it's slimy in there. Can a glass eye cry? And how funny it is that I can see the glass eye but the glass eye can't see me.

'Because he always believes me. Because I'm his father. Whatever you tell him, he won't believe you.'

Now I can see four glass eyes. One of them on his forehead, blurry, as if it was getting further and further away.

'Paul and your dad are so stupid,' says Granddad. 'They wouldn't understand, they'd think there's something wrong with you, but I understand you, I know what's going on inside of you.'

I can feel his breath on me, on my cheeks; a dull, musty smell.

'You're all muddled up, little Malvina,' he says,

stroking my head very gently and tenderly, and he's right, everything inside me is messed up, in complete chaos, a room that's been ransacked and left behind – there are clothes lying around, books, pieces of paper and old exercise books, and I'm standing next to it all and I'm supposed to tidy up, while it keeps getting messed up all over again.

'I'm right aren't I, Malvina? You don't know how wonderful love is, that's why you think such terrible things about your granddad. I can't believe it, such terrible things even though I love you so much…'

He presses me back against the sofa, and the glass eyes blur together into a grey, wavering mass that flows towards me and twines itself around me like a sea monster, like a giant octopus. A giant octopus latching onto me with its suckers. One on my mouth sucks my breath out of me and presses its breath into me, a grey tongue licking across my lips.

'You like that, don't you, Malvina? You must like it,' he says and kisses me, shaking.

Something strange happens. I feel myself with-drawing from my body. Slowly, first from my legs, then from my tummy, going further and further up. I disappear.

I disappear into my head.

I hear his voice from a long way away.

'You promised,' he says over and over, and I can't think what he means.

All I can see are clouds drifting past my eyes, the same ones as outside only much bigger and softer, and

I realise I'm sitting right behind my eyes. Very tiny, hidden. No one will find me here, I think with relief, and then he says, 'You promised your gran, you know, you remember, you and Gran last May...'

He takes his old hands off me, shakes me because I'm not moving, pushes me off the couch as if he were suddenly angry with me. I pull myself together and stumble into the bathroom. It's not easy walking when you're sitting behind your eyes.

'Did you sort it all out?' asks Dad when he comes to pick me up.

Granddad puts his hand on the back of my neck. I can tell what that means.

Keep your mouth shut, it means.

'Of course,' he says. 'Malvina's a clever girl.'

Then he lets me go.

Everything's quiet at the villa.

Very quiet. Screwy's not here yet. I just drop my bike on the ground by the gap in the fence and run through the garden, through the supple dried grass and the kicked-in door and then up the stairs, up to the attic.

I tear the pink curtain down from the ceiling; it's easy enough. It sails down like an empty hot-air balloon, swathing me like a bride's veil.

'It's so ugly,' Lizzy said when I hung it up.

She was hanging upside down from a beam, the beam behind her knees, and I said, 'You'll go stupid if the blood flows to your brain for too long,' because Lizzy was pretty red in the face already from hanging upside-down, and then she said her times tables as she was hanging, to prove it doesn't make you go stupid.

I stomp up and down on my mattress, stamping so long that the cover rips and foam comes swelling out.

And here's Screwy. He's standing very still in the hatch, watching me rant and rage, watching me tear my attic apart.

'What're you staring at?' I shout, hearing my voice break as I speak.

It's not really my voice. It's the wild buzzing of hornets in my ears. He can't know that but I know it, and I know it doesn't sound like shouting – it's too quiet. My voice is quiet and scratchy, as if I'd swallowed sand. I can tell by his face that he's not taking me seriously. They never do because I can't shout properly, not like Lizzy; she can shout down the whole street if she feels like it, and she often does feel like it when she's angry. Lizzy says it must be my vocal chords, but I know I just don't have the guts.

'You can bugger off!' I shout anyway and carry on throwing.

Another cushion and another one, and then candles, red lumps of wax that shatter when they hit the wooden floor, covering it in red splinters.

'You did come after all,' he says

I stop for a moment, feeling a blush shoot to my cheeks.

'Looks like it, doesn't it, but I didn't come because of you,' I say. 'Not because of you, so there's no need to let it go to your head.'

Screwy nods.

'I thought you weren't going to come,' he says.

He takes a step towards me, the wax crunching beneath his soles. A gust of wind blows through the holes in the roof. It's April, scraps of cloud are floating across the sky, letting the sun shine out for a moment and casting fast-moving shadows across my face.

'Leave me alone!' I shout at him again. 'Just leave me alone.'

The curtain has got tangled around my feet. I kick it loose, kicking out like crazy. I don't care what he thinks of me as long as he leaves me in peace and gets out of here, as long as he doesn't touch me.

'What's the matter with you?' he asks.

For a moment an image flashes into my mind, just for a fraction of a second, blindingly bright, so bright it hurts. I see my gran, her white wavy hair stuck to her head like tissue paper, turned to ringlets by her sweat, and her weak pale face with its wrinkled lips. I see her so clearly, holding my hand. She's pressing as hard as she can and that's not very hard, it's like trying to shake hands with a mouse. That's what I thought, as if I had a mouse's paw in my hand.

'Nothing's the matter,' I shout. 'You can't get it into your head, can you?'

He takes another uncertain step, shoving his hands into his pockets as if he were looking for stones in them, and when he doesn't find any he shoves them even deeper and clenches his fists.

'Why are you smashing everything up?' he asks.

The mattress gives way under my kicking feet, like walking on clouds, clouds of crumbling foam and torn material.

'They're tearing this wreck down soon too,' I mimic him, perfectly imitating his tone of voice, slightly bored, not bothered; I can almost feel the cigarette hanging from the corner of my lips.

'And now get out of here!' I say.

I search the attic with my eyes for something to throw. There are roof tiles lying around and loose boards with rusty nails in them. Not even Lizzy would throw something like that. She wouldn't dare, I know, because her mother told us we'd be in big trouble if we went too far with the boys. *Going too far* meant you mustn't really hurt anyone, not even if you're really angry. She said you can let your anger out on anything, just not on people, animals and plants, and we stuck to that as far as we could. Lizzy would never throw roof tiles. Never in her life.

Carefully, as if the floor was covered in broken glass, as if the red splinters weren't just candle wax, he picks his way back to the stairs. Even though I'm not holding a tile in my hand, or a board with a rusty nail in it.

He disappears through the hatch, his hands still in his pockets. Looks like he's never heard you're not supposed to go down steps with your hands in your pockets, that Screwy.

When I think he's gone, he shouts up at me 'What's your name?' He's at the bottom, right downstairs outside the house where he kicked the door in last year, by now. Gone for good.

'Malvina,' I whisper so quietly that he can't possibly hear me.

'My name's Malvina,' I whisper in my voice, buzzing like a thousand hornets.

Tuesday

The boys didn't dare come right up to the villa to start with. They stopped up on the hill just behind the estate and stared over at us through binoculars. Lizzy and I hid behind the windows, and I said, 'Why don't they come over here?'

'Maybe they think there's loads of us,' Lizzy whispered, and peeped out over the windowsill, just a bit so the boys didn't get her in their sights.

Behind the estate is a circle of sand, and they rode their bikes round and round there with their binoculars around their necks. We could even tell them apart from a distance, mainly because Screwy used to spend most of the time riding on his back wheel.

'What a show-off,' Lizzy said.

And we could tell Hubba Bubba because his bike was much too small, a yellow folding bike even we would have been ashamed of.

'I wouldn't be caught dead riding a bike like that,' Lizzy said.

I raised the objection that my bike wasn't much better, but Lizzy wasn't having any of it. At least mine wasn't yellow.

After half an hour the boys headed back to the estate, and Lizzy and I held a powwow about what to do next. We had an ominous hunch that the boys wouldn't stay on their estate where they belonged – boys are predictable like that, they always do what makes the most trouble, so Lizzy said we should arm ourselves for the worst.

'You can bet they'll be down here tomorrow,' she said.

I didn't want to bet on that at all. I'd much rather they just left us in peace.

Lizzy didn't want to bet either, she wanted to get down to business. The two of us crept around the villa laying traps.

'They mustn't even get as far as the villa,' she said, planting a rake on the path to the house with its prongs up. Where the grass was especially long and thick.

'Well, what do you think?' she said. 'You can't see it at all.'

And then we imagined the boys coming to the villa the next day, single file, Screwy the show-off first of all. Marching up the path one by one and then Screwy treading on the rake.

'Ouch,' I said, falling back onto the grass next to the rake.

'They won't come back after that,' Lizzy said. 'Believe you me.'

The next day we rushed to the villa as early as possible so we wouldn't miss the show when the boys walked into our trap. We hid our bikes in the field to give them a false sense of security. We slipped through the gap in the fence one by one, first me and then Lizzy, and that's how we went up the path, quickly so no one would see us.

'Hey hey!' Lizzy said behind me and then she didn't say anything, because then she trod on the rake. It made a short whirring sound in the air and then a dull thud, and when I turned round Lizzy was lying on her back on the grass and holding one eye.

'Shit,' she groaned, very muffled, and that was much worse than her usual screaming.

I was used to that, but the whole thing's much more worrying if Lizzy doesn't scream and shout when she's angry or in pain. I knelt down next to her, on the grass by the rake.

'Oh God, Lizzy,' I said, 'are you all right?' And Lizzy rocked to and fro, her hands pressed to her face.

'Oh, oh, oh,' she said, and I was really glad there was no blood coming out from beneath her hands. I'd expected her to be all covered in blood under them.

'Maybe it wasn't such a good idea with the rake after all,' I said carefully and waited for her to stop saying *oh, oh, oh*.

'Don't you tell anybody,' she said then, even before

she took her hands off her face. 'Especially not my mum, she'd kill me, you know, *do as you would be done by* and all that.'

When she took her hands away I had to tell her if her eye was still there, and to be honest I couldn't really tell all that well because her eyelid was incredibly swollen, so fat you couldn't say whether her eye was there or not.

'Ummm,' I said, 'I think so,' and then Lizzy started crying because she might only have one eye, and I thought that was really bad too. Only having one eye probably isn't much fun.

She dragged herself into the villa, into the bathroom in front of the broken old cabinet. We stood there and watched her eye gradually turning blue. Not just a little bit – dark blue and purple at the edges. To cheer her up I said she could wear an eye patch, a black one, but then she really started crying.

Of course, the boys had to choose that day to come over to the villa from the estate. We could hear the clattering of their bikes outside the garden fence.

'Quick,' Lizzy said and wiped the tears brusquely from her face. 'Get me the rake!'

Mrs Bitschek's flat smells of cinnamon and cigarettes; I was in there a couple of years ago, waiting in her kitchen until Gran got back from shopping. Gran liked Mrs Bitschek too but she said we mustn't tell Granddad or he'd get angry, so we didn't tell him I'd waited in her kitchen when Gran was late.

As I run up the stairs to Granddad's flat today her front door is open. It smells of cinnamon and cigarette smoke again and I can hear Mrs Bitschek tidying up inside. She's talking to her baby in Polish, but then she says, 'You can come on in,' and I nearly die of shock because she can't possibly see me. But I put my basket down outside the door and take a couple of cautious steps into the hall. The television is on in the living room, her oldest son is lying on his front watching Japanese mangas, and the other children are playing outside. 'I'm just making coffee,' says Mrs Bitschek. 'Do you want one?'

I nod and follow her into the kitchen, stepping over abandoned Lego scattered across the floor, and sit down at the kitchen table underneath a huge picture of two angels in a golden frame.

'They're guardian angels,' says Mrs Bitschek when she sees me looking at it, and pours water into two little cups; she's put the baby down with the Lego. 'Don't want to go to Granddad?' she says, giving me a big smile so that I see her gold teeth flashing. 'Never mind, sweetie, it's nice here too.'

I smile back and sip at my coffee; I never usually drink coffee, I normally think it tastes disgusting, but this coffee tastes different, very sweet and sticky, and it's black, deep black, and there are crumbs of coffee floating in the cup. Mrs Bitschek says it's Turkish coffee, you only drink a little bit because it awakens your spirits. And if they get woken too much you can't do anything but dance all day long till your feet are sore. It happened to her once, she says, and she danced for three days and three nights, and then she couldn't walk properly for three weeks. She grins at me again and I get the feeling she's fibbing, but I only take tiny sips just in case, so I don't end up dancing. Dusty sunlight falls through the windows. The flat is brighter than Granddad's because it faces the street and not the shady back yard, but it's much more noisy to make up for it – you can hear cars and delivery vans and the people walking past the window talking. If you listen carefully you can make out every word they say, but I guess Mrs Bitschek doesn't care because her baby's usually screaming most of the time anyway. He's quiet now, sitting on the floor among the Lego and sucking at a piece of bread he found under the table. My mum would flip out if she saw that; it must be very unhygienic but the baby looks happy enough. Next to the baby lies a huge rusty-red tom-cat, looking at me out of narrow slits of eyes.

'Watch out for Bratko,' says Mrs Bitschek when I stretch out my hand to the cat, and he promptly hisses at me and claws in my direction.

'He's a devil,' she says. 'He's next life of my uncle, was very bad man.'

She shakes her head sadly.

'How often I say, "Mary mother of God, why you send back my Uncle Bratko? Why not good person?" But no answer.'

She shakes her head again and sips at her Turkish coffee.

I shift furtively away from the cat but I don't let him out of my sight. He blinks, then rolls himself up again between the Lego.

'Why don't you chase him away?' I ask.

Bratko gives a moody wave of his tail. He doesn't look like the kind of cat you could chase away.

'Oh no,' says Mrs Bitschek, 'you chase cat out of house, you chase luck out of house. Anyway you have to look after your relatives.'

She sighs and knocks back the rest of her coffee in one go.

'When you've finished you do like this,' she says and turns her cup upside-down on the saucer. Using her left hand, she waves the cup in a circle three times and says some Polish words, then she puts the saucer down on the table and puts the cup down next to it with care.

'You see,' she says, 'like this I read future from coffee grounds.'

'Many babies,' she says, patting her stomach. I can't tell anything much of course, apart from the fact that she obviously does have lots of babies; the youngest one is dribbling on his crust of bread and babbling away unintelligibly.

Slightly suspicious, I sway my cup around in a circle too, repeat the strange words Mrs Bitschek patiently pronounces, then I cautiously reveal the coffee grounds. They're stuck to the saucer like a little black cake.

'Aha,' says Mrs Bitschek. 'In love!'

I turn bright red again and lower my eyes. What a load of rubbish – me, in love!

She pokes about in the dark crumbs with the back end of her spoon, her friendly face furrowed by deep lines.

'Dark clouds,' she says, not looking at me. She turns the saucer in all directions, watching a thin trickle of coffee spreading across the china.

'Very dark clouds, here young man, sunshine, there…someone else, dark clouds, must watch out, someone wants bad things.' She says and puts the saucer back on the table. 'Oh, don't get shock,' she says and pats me on the hand. 'You're strong girl.'

Then she points her spoon at the window behind her. 'Look out there,' she says, 'but be careful!'

I creep up to the window and peek out through a gap in the net curtains. Down on the street, Screwy is turning his circles. He rides round once on his back wheel like last year, the chippings on the road crunching under his tyre.

'How did you know?' I whisper, really impressed.

'Oh him, he's down there all along,' she says innocently. 'I saw him before.'

We grin at each other. She has huge yellow teeth – not even Pearl Drops would help.

'Off you run,' she says, 'I'll give your granddad the basket.'

'Honest?' I say, feeling a huge smile spreading out

from my stomach, over my neck, my chin, my whole face. I jump up and run out of the flat, down the stairs, onto the street. My bike sparkles in the sun and I can hear Screwy calling me.

'Hey, Miss Moody!' he shouts.

Then we ride alongside each other in harmony. As we cycle out of the yard I think I can feel Granddad's eyes on my back, but I don't care – I'm a strong girl, at least at the moment; I pedal a bit faster to get rid of the unpleasant feeling he's causing in my back. When we turn the next corner all there is is sunshine and blue sky. We head straight for the Italian ice-cream parlour, a tiny bar with light-blue and pink fifties tiles and cast-iron banisters on the steps outside, where you can sit to eat your ice cream. Screwy buys an ice-cream sundae with two spoons for us to share, and the man who serves us makes stupid comments, *grande amore* and that kind of thing, winking at Screwy with his thumbs up. I can't help suspecting Screwy must come here often. Then we sit down on the steps, pigeons all around us again waiting for a bite of our food, and Screwy tells me not to take any notice of the stupid guy, he always talks crap because he gets bored working in his ice-cream parlour all day long. I don't care anyway; I lean back on my elbows and savour the taste of vanilla ice cream and strawberry sauce.

'The cream's the best bit,' says Screwy. 'It freezes into little lumps.'

We both try the cream in the middle and agree

that the stupid ice-cream man sells the world's best sundaes, even if he's not quite right in the head.

The steps under my bum are still really cold – my mum would say I'll get piles. You're not allowed to sit on the floor in April and you're not allowed to go barefoot either, because there's an R in the month. But luckily my mother can't see me now; she's probably lying in the darkened living room listening to quiet classical music while my father mows the lawn outside. When he comes in the house later he'll moan about always having to do everything himself and it being my mother's fault our family's falling apart. He says that a lot, sometimes I can hear them fighting at night. He says: 'We could be much better off if you'd pull yourself together at long last,' and she cries and says her head is bursting, it's his fault her head is bursting. Then I pull the cover up over my head so I don't have to listen any more.

'You're funny, you are,' says Screwy out of nowhere.

He's scraping the last remains of ice cream carefully out of the cup with his plastic spoon, not looking at me, and my brain starts turning circles because I know it's true. And I don't know how to explain why I throw lumps of wax at him and chase him out of the villa one day and the next day I'm sitting in the sun with him outside the ice-cream parlour. So I say, 'You're funny too' – because attack is the best form of defence.

'No I'm not,' he says.

He throws the cup and the spoon along with it in the bin, which is at least three metres away from us.

'Well you're an incredible show-off then,' I say, rolling my eyes.

Some kids run past us up the stairs, bumping into us. Screwy slides closer to me until our thighs are touching. I can hear the ice-cream man joking with the kids. They want lemon sorbet, one scoop each. The money jingles on the counter and my head rushes and my legs tingle. I look down at myself, my thin legs in dark jeans next to Screwy's legs with holes in his trousers again, you can see his knees and little golden blond hairs. I don't know what to do with my hands so I fold my arms, and I don't know whether I want him to move away again or stay where he is.

'Hmm,' he says, 'you gotta give the girls something to look at.'

'Aha,' I say, 'so that's why you were so awful to us last year, is it? I can think of better things to look at.'

I bite my tongue – I couldn't have said anything more stupid. Well at least Lizzy would be proud of me, but that's not much consolation. Screwy doesn't say anything, just fiddles around with his trainers. It looks like he doesn't feel like talking about last year.

Just as the silence between us is starting to get unbearable, I spot my sister Anne cycling towards us. She's got a mountain bike, a brand-new one, the kind where you have to lean forward to hold onto the handlebars, and that's what she's doing. I have to add that Anne's also got pretty big breasts, and right now she's wearing a little top with spaghetti straps, her iPod hanging round her neck and her blonde hair blowing in the wind. Oh my God! Just what I need right now.

She stops right in front of us.

'There you are,' she says, looking curiously from me to Screwy and back again. You can hear the bass booming out of her earphones.

'Dad's looking for you,' she says with glee. 'Granddad's in an evil mood because Mrs Bitschek took his lunch round, and Dad's in an evil mood because Granddad's in an evil mood. You've got one huge telling-off coming to you.'

She blinks at Screwy with her mascara-rimmed owl eyes. I could strangle her!

'So?' I say, because I can't think of anything better to say again, and anyway I don't want to make a fool of myself in front of Screwy. He's already pulling a pretty strange face, although I can't quite tell if he thinks my sister is great or really awful. But most boys think Anne is great because she's got big breasts and blonde hair and wears mini-skirts to school that hardly come down over her bum and freshens up her lipstick at break time. Dark red! Once I caught a load of boys from my class hanging around the window outside Anne's classroom, just because there was a rumour going round school that she was wearing a cropped top and a sports bra that day. I wondered what was so special about that. When I asked them the boys just said, 'Hey, she's a babe!' Which made it perfectly clear that I wasn't a babe.

'If I was you I'd head home right now,' she says. And when I don't make a move: 'Go on, get going!'

She gets back on her bike and rides in a circle, presumably so that Screwy can admire her from all sides.

'If I was you I'd bugger off,' I say, angry now. Screwy's still fiddling with his trainers but I can see he's grinning. He presses his leg against mine, and I press back and all of a sudden I feel really good and really cool. I blow my fringe off my forehead. The kids run back past us down the steps, one of them drops his ice cream on the pavement and starts to cry. 'No, no, no,' he screams, and the ice-cream man comes running out of the shop to console him.

'I'll give you a new one, don't worry,' he says.

My sister turns her bike round, plugs her earphones into her ears and speeds off.

'Cute guy,' she shouts over her shoulder, although I'm not quite sure whether she means Screwy or the ice-cream guy.

'That was my sister,' I say, which is a pretty superfluous comment. 'She's pretty dumb,' I add.

'You don't say,' says Screwy. 'I'd never have noticed.'

I pull myself up by the banisters, bouncing on my heels indecisively.

'Come to the villa tomorrow if you want,' I say. 'I've gotta go home now and get my telling-off.'

wednesday

That day, as the boys dropped their bikes on the grass outside the villa, I ran outside and got the rake. Lizzy took it and looked me firmly in my two eyes with her one eye. 'Whatever happens,' she whispered, 'don't say a word, and don't come out. Promise!'

I promised and watched her in awe. She was going to sacrifice herself, for us, for the villa. I'd never seen anything so heroic, it gave me goose pimples all up my arms. I was so proud to have a friend as courageous as Lizzy. She turned round and went out, the rake over her shoulder, looking very brave and determined. For a moment she stood in the doorway, blinded by the bright light of the summer afternoon, a dark silhouette with a spear resting in her right hand, and then the door fell to behind her and I grabbed hold of the handle tightly, with my ear to the wood. By now the boys were marching along the path to the house in single file, Screwy at the front, then Poker Face, Puddle and Hubba Bubba. The grass, parched by the summer, crunched beneath their feet; other than that, there wasn't a sound to be heard. The heat crept into every nook and cranny. Soon the sun would be at its highest point in the sky, and I felt my anger coming back again because I couldn't help thinking of our old frog pond where these brats' houses were now. I looked round for something to use as a weapon in case anything happened, but there was nothing but a dented saucepan, so I pressed my ear to the wood again and listened.

'Stop!' said Lizzy. 'Don't go one step further.'

The boys stopped and stared, as Lizzy told me later, horrified by her face. They were maybe five metres away. Lizzy swung the rake off her shoulder and planted it between herself and the boys.

'I wouldn't get in his bad books today,' she said in a low, threatening voice, and I stood behind the door wondering what she meant, and the boys were wondering too because they couldn't see anyone apart from Lizzy.

'Who are you talking about?' asked Screwy, gesturing with one hand for the others to stay where they were, and they exchanged confused looks. It gradually started dawning on me what Lizzy was thinking, but if her plan backfired...I didn't want to even think about what would happen if the boys caught on and came crashing in. I smothered a giggle and swore, because I couldn't see anything and I'd have given anything to see Screwy's face, and the others' of course.

'Weeell,' said Lizzy slowly, 'take a look at my face. I shouldn't have got in his way today.'

She left a meaningful pause, then she held up the rake; with a little goodwill you could just make out a couple of drops of blood on the end of the handle.

'Catch!' she said, throwing the rake to Screwy, who caught it in midair with a dextrous grab.

'Our leader's in a bloody bad mood today,' she said as the boys passed the rake around between them. 'I'd say you should make yourselves scarce...'

She didn't finish her sentence, turning round and slipping in through the door. The two of us ran upstairs into Evil Frederick's living room; that was where we had the best view. We squatted down by the windowsill and peered through the broken pane. The boys were still standing around in confusion, discussing what to do. They kept throwing glances over their shoulders at the door, but unfortunately we couldn't make out a word they were saying.

'They can't really be that dumb,' I whispered, holding my hand in front of my mouth so I didn't laugh out loud.

'Oh yes, they can,' said Lizzy. 'It's worse than we thought... Honest, I never thought it'd work.'

Outside, the boys turned on their heels. We watched them until they disappeared between the fields.

'Gimme five!' said Lizzy, dropping down onto her bottom because her legs had gone to sleep from squatting for so long.

Later Lizzy's mother took the photo with the eye patch; we'd found it in Lizzy's old dressing-up box and she'd decided to wear it for the next few weeks. In fact she was still wearing the patch for ages, even after her eye was better.

Bratko is waiting for me when I turn into the back yard. He rolls to and fro on the asphalt, warmed by the sun, stretching his marmalade tummy out towards me.

'I'm not falling for your tricks,' I say as I jump off my bike.

He gives an indignant meow and walks ahead of me to the doorway, where he stops and pees against the wood.

'If Granddad saw you,' I say to him, tempted to reach my hand out to him again.

Upstairs, I catch sight of Mrs Bitschek's chubby frame. She's fiddling with something outside the door to Granddad's flat, and she jumps when she sees me.

'Holy Mary!' she says, 'you give me a shock.'

She hides her hands behind her back quick as a flash, pressing past me to her flat.

'What're you doing there?' I ask. I can make out a movement behind the spy-hole in Granddad's door; he must be watching us.

Mrs Bitschek beckons me over, still hiding one hand behind her back.

'Just salt,' she whispers.

'What,' I whisper back, 'just salt?'

Bratko rubs up against my trouser leg and I'm scared he'll bite my toes – I'm wearing sandals for the first time this year.

'I sprinkle salt on threshold,' Mrs Bitschek whispers. 'Drives out evil spirits.'

'Aha,' I whisper. 'And does it work?'

She gives a hefty nod; she's wearing a pale-pink headscarf with curlers underneath.

'You must do it when moon is waning, then it works well,' she whispers.

She picks up Bratko with her free hand and presses the struggling cat to her generous bosom.

Granddad is pretty cross with me. He doesn't say a word as I put the food Mum gave me for him into the fridge. I take my time; I like the kitchen. It's small with brightly coloured curtains in front of the shelves that my gran made. She always used to say: 'Back then when you weren't even a twinkle in your daddy's eye.' She meant she made the curtains before I was born; they're blue with red and yellow roses and they match the pale-blue kitchen cupboards.

Sometimes I think, there were so many years when I wasn't born. It's a funny thought, I know, and it's really hard to explain as well. Every now and then Lizzy and I talk about the past, because we only met four years ago so there are lots of things we don't know about each other. Lizzy has loads of funny stories to tell, about her and her mother and all the things she got up to, about the time the priest gave her a slap round the ear for climbing on the font, all that kind of thing. And then Lizzy tells me to think of a funny story from before we met, and the strange thing is – I can't think of anything. Or almost; it feels like opening a photo album that's strewn over and over with hundreds of blind spots. You can still make the odd thing out, half-images, torn pictures, but no proper memories, at least no funny stories. And that scares me and I get a queasy feeling all through my body, a slight tingling that spreads out from the back of my forehead, further and further until my whole body tingles and tingles like crazy. I usually say I just haven't had any funny experiences, and I jump up so the tingling stops. The best way to make it go away is to run really fast until you're out of breath.

I put milk and butter in Granddad's fridge and then I go into the living room. Granddad is sitting in an armchair in front of the window, looking at me without a word as I stand in the doorway.

'Well then,' I say. 'I'll be going then.'

My heart is beating really fast, I can hear it again. The strange tingling is spreading out in my head and behind my forehead; now I know what the tingling is – I didn't realise for all those years. The tingling is fear, terrible fear.

'I'm disappointed in you, Malvina,' says Grand-dad. 'I thought I could count on you.'

I lean my shoulder against the doorframe – I'm suddenly scared the floor will give way beneath me; it's swaying slightly and Granddad looks really blurred, like looking at someone through frosted glass.

He talks and talks, on and on, about Gran, that Gran's counting on me up in heaven, that she's looking down on us and must be crying now because I've been leaving my granddad alone and sending the Polish lady with his food.

'What will they think?' he says. 'They'll think there's something the matter with us.'

He pauses for a moment and rests his gaze on me. I twist the handle of my basket between my fingers and try to focus on a spot on the carpet. The carpet is dark red with square black patterns and tassels on the ends. I used to comb them and plait them together. How stupid, I think.

'What's happened to your friend Lizzy?' he says.

I just shrug; I don't want to tell Granddad she's gone on holiday. It's none of his business. He says Lizzy's bad company for a girl like me because her parents are divorced, and people shouldn't do that. People shouldn't get divorced. 'Remember that,' he told me once. 'You have to stay together until you die.' I thought it was spooky, all that *till death us do part*; it always gave me goose pimples and I could understand why Lizzy's mother was having none of it. Lizzy always says her father used to be a real tyrant, and then he ran off with his secretary. Her name's Annabelle and she's twenty-three – twenty years younger than Lizzy's dad. Sometimes Lizzy has to go to lunch at her dad and Annabelle's place. She says Annabelle acts like she is her mother when she's round there, and Lizzy can't stand that. Lizzy's mother hasn't got a new boyfriend, and Lizzy thinks maybe she'll turn into a lesbian because she's always hanging out with her best girlfriend, but then I said that's rubbish, then we'd be lesbians too, and Lizzy said it'd be cool if her mum was a lesbian, it's something special – not everyone has a lesbian mum.

'What about her?' I say.

Granddad keeps staring at me.

'Nothing, nothing,' he says, smiling slightly as if he knows something I don't know.

'Friendships like that aren't for ever,' he says. 'All of a sudden you'll be left on your own when Lizzy gets a boyfriend. That can happen quickly nowadays.'

I don't know what he's getting at; all I know is that the floor, the red carpet with its tassels and the whole room are starting to sway more and more, the longer Granddad talks at me. In the end everything turns a somersault and all I can see is black; all I can hear is the bang as the back of my head smashes against the table in the hall with the telephone on it.

I'm still lying on the couch when Dad comes to pick me up. He has grass cuttings on his shoes from mowing the lawn. I can hear him talking to Granddad in the hall. Granddad says I just fell over and he thinks it's a trick. He's whispering but I can still make out every word, and I wonder how he imagines a trick like that – I mean, no one bangs their head on a telephone table for fun. Dad's not convinced either, he says he hopes I'm not going to turn out like my mother. He means her migraines. He couldn't stand another one with migraines in the house.

And then I jump up from the couch. My head still hurts a bit where I fell against the edge, but otherwise I'm fine.

'I haven't got a migraine,' I say, 'and I can go home on my own.'

I've just remembered all of a sudden that Screwy might be coming to the villa, so I can't go letting my father ferry me around.

Slightly self-conscious, we all face each other in the hall, surrounded by family photos in gold frames; most of them are of me as a six-year-old, looking into the camera with a serious face. Sometimes I look as if I was somewhere else; I can remember that feeling of being somewhere else. My head throbs as I push past my father to the door.

'Thanks for coming to pick me up,' I say, and then I'm out of the door.

We meet by chance between the fields on the way to the villa. There's not much growing there yet.

In summer they're all full of corn and wheat and rye, you can build passageways and mazes and hide. Not any more of course, I'm not a little kid any more, but it was always great in the fields. We push our bikes alongside one another because Screwy's got a flat tyre. I tell him to just leave his bike where it is, but he's scared it'll get nicked.

We push them over the next hill and once we're at the top we can see down onto the villa. Outside are cars, two big cars, and there are men walking around.

'Oh no,' I say. 'They can't start yet!'

Now we do just leave our bikes on the ground. I lock Screwy's bike to mine so he doesn't have to worry, and then we creep closer. We tread through a freshly ploughed field all the way along a white-blossoming blackthorn hedge to the next field. The birds in the hedge are loud, swarming out ahead of us. Screwy creeps ducked down ahead of me, his hair bouncing at every step. We squat behind the garden fence in a little ditch overgrown with weeds. We have a good view of the men through the gaps in the fence. They're surveyors – I know that because Lizzy's dad does the same sort of thing, he's the one who tells the surveyors where to do their surveying. They've got funny instruments with them that look like telescopes on tripods, and one of them keeps scribbling on a big dark-brown clipboard.

There are men inside the villa too, we can see their shapes spooking around behind the empty holes of windows. Why does it have to happen now, when

Lizzy's not here? I've no idea what Lizzy could do about these men tearing down the villa and everything, but even her just being here would make me feel better. If Lizzy was here now we'd hold hands and make plans for stopping the demolition, I'm sure we would.

Stones are boring into my knee and my head still hurts.

'Something the matter?' Screwy whispers.

He gives me a searching look as I'm shuffling about uncomfortably and can't find a comfortable position for my legs.

'You're all pale in the face.'

That's just how I feel right now. Pale.

'No, I'm fine,' I say. 'I just hit my head on a telephone table, everything else is OK.'

'God, you've probably got concussion. You really are crazy.'

He leans his back against the fence. We can't see the men like this but it's much more comfy. I do the same, stretching out my legs and wriggling my bare toes in my sandals.

'Pins and needles!' I say, and move them around a bit more so they wake up.

'How did it happen?' asks Screwy. He's digging around in his pockets for his cigarettes again, and when he finds them half of them have crumbled away.

'Stupid question,' I say. 'I always get pins and needles from squatting down like that.'

'Not your toes, you idiot, I mean your head.'

The men shout something behind us; it sounds like they're hammering around at the villa, maybe to find out the best way to tear it down.

'Oh right,' I say, thinking about what to tell him – I don't want to say I passed out.

'I tripped over.'

Screwy lights his cigarette. He doesn't ask me any more if I want one but that's better anyway – my parents would flip out if I came home smelling of smoke. Cigarettes give you lung cancer, they say, and smoker's legs and yellow teeth. My pigeons fly their circles above us. They'll have to move out too. Maybe they've got a nice flat in town, I think, but what about me – where am I supposed to go?

I slip down a bit until I'm lying on my back, as my bum's falling asleep too now and the sun's shining right in my face. I close my eyes and fold my arms behind my head.

'You don't want to tell me your name,' says Screwy.

I shake my head without opening my eyes; I don't even know why myself. Probably because of Lizzy, because of our oath.

'It's a secret,' I say.

'All right, then,' says Screwy. 'Then mine's a secret too.'

His voice sounds offended; I can't help grinning.

'I know your name already,' I say. Screwy takes a drag on his cigarette, I can see it glowing.

'Right, you know mine already,' he says, and his voice sounds even more offended than before.

'Yeah, your name's Screwy,' I say, cool as a cucumber.

We hear car doors slamming; it sounds like the men have finished their surveying. An engine starts, purring quietly as the car makes a complicated turn on the narrow road. The other driver doesn't even try, just reverses up the track.

'You're crazy,' he says.

The cars disappear in clouds of dust and then it's quiet again, and we get back onto our feet and crawl through a gap in the fence. The men have left strange poles behind in the ground and there are a couple of rolls of red and white barrier tape in front of the villa, like they use on building sites. We look around every room but nothing's changed in the villa, not yet, just the smell of the men. It smells of city and aftershave and cigarettes. I wrinkle my nose in disgust. We go right to the top but it smells just the same as usual up there, of wood and feathers and fresh air.

It's nice up here with Screwy. I like it when he's here. I like it when we lean against the beams together and talk. I forget the men and that the villa's going to be torn down soon. Screwy thinks up names for me like for Rumpelstiltskin; he says a name and I shake my head, not letting him wear me down.

'Sophie,' he says. 'Maria, Joanne, Esther, Juliet...'

He can't stop now.

'Ermintrude, Sarah, Hannah, Elsie...'

We laugh and I shake my head.

'You'll never guess,' I say. 'Forget it.'

He puts his arm round me, around my shoulders, but I wriggle out of it; I can't stand arms around my shoulders. They give me goose pimples.

'What's up with you?' he says.

'Nothing,' I say. 'Just leave it.'

He doesn't try again but he gives me a very funny look.

'I just don't like it,' I say, feeling like I ought to explain myself.

The pigeons coo above our heads. Everything would be peaceful if the tingling in my legs hadn't started again. I climb up into the beams to distract myself; Screwy watches me from below, making a friendly face, the friendliest face I've ever seen. He doesn't ask questions, he's just there and watching me, and I climb into the beams, higher and higher.

When he's there I'm not scared of falling.

Thursday

Gran came out of hospital for the first time not long after I started school. She wore a headscarf because she had lost all her hair and she didn't want me to be scared of her. Of course I knew she'd lost all her hair, every single one. The two of us were standing in the little kitchen, the little pale-blue kitchen with the brightly coloured curtains.

'What's a cancer?' I asked her, and Gran dropped the plate she was holding back into the sink, and the dishwater splashed in all directions, onto my face and her apron.

Cancer. I'd heard the word the day before from my parents. My mother had said the cancer would eat Gran up from within, and I thought it must be possible to find a cancer like that inside my gran. I was sure they must be doing something wrong, the people at the hospital just didn't know what to do with a cancer.

Gran wiped her hands on her apron and sat down on the floor with me. That was quite hard for her because of her joints, but when Granddad wasn't there we often sat on the kitchen floor, leaning against the pale-blue kitchen cupboards. We usually told each other silly things we thought up and inspected Gran's varicose veins under her tights. I thought varicose veins were a wonderful thing, a mysterious thing, something you could see even though they belonged on the inside of the body.

'Is it true the cancer's eating you up from the inside?' I asked in a quiet voice, tracing one of the varicose veins with my forefinger, a particularly thick one that branched off into more and more knobbles; if you pressed it with your finger it swelled up, but I didn't do that because Gran had said varicose veins weren't a laughing matter.

'Yes, it's true,' said Gran just as quietly and pulled me towards her shoulder, hugging me and kissing my forehead like she did when I was crying or when Dad came to pick me up.

'The cancer,' she said, 'has been inside me for a long time. For years. It starts out just a thought, a feeling, an unhappy feeling, a little wound where someone hurts you, and if you don't make sure you heal the wound then something grows out of it, it gets bigger and bigger and then you're eaten up from the inside because you didn't watch out for yourself and the little cut all those years. Because you were unhappy for all those years.'

I felt the scratchy fabric of her blouse and her bony shoulder under my cheek. The soap suds collapsed with a crackling sound, a quiet bursting of rainbow bubbles; I wished I could have just jumped up and sunk my arms into the foam up to my elbows, as if that would wash away everything she'd said and the cancer and everything that seemed to be looming ahead of us so ominously.

'What do you do with a wound like that?' I asked her. I couldn't picture anything, nothing real, maybe something like a cut in your soul, something tiny and pale, something you can't see from the outside, that you only feel when you're lying in bed on your own at night and listening hard to yourself. Then you might hear your heart beating at first, and then behind the beating you'd feel something else, the cut, or maybe it's just a bruise, a scrape, a scratch.

'You have to listen to it,' said Gran. 'And you mustn't stop until it's said its last word.'

'I never listened, Malvina,' she said.

A sound on the staircase made us sit upright. Mrs Bitschek had moved into the building back then but there weren't any other children because she was only pregnant with her first baby. She'd come over from Poland pregnant, if you like. It was usually quiet because the people upstairs and downstairs from my grandparents were old too and didn't make any noise. Gran thought it was a shame there were no children for me to play with, she said there was nothing more cheerful than children's laughter. But what we heard wasn't laughter; we heard a crash as if someone had fallen over on the stairs, and Gran went white in the face, even whiter than she was already.

'Granddad's drunk,' she said, getting to her feet, climbing over my legs and closing the kitchen door, very fast. She turned the key in the lock. The crashing got louder and we heard Granddad swearing because he couldn't get the key in the keyhole. Up until that day Granddad had never been drunk, at least not when I was visiting. He'd once told me he kept a list, he drew a line for every glass of red wine so that he always knew how much he'd drunk. 'Sometimes I get a bit muddled up,' he'd said, winking at me, 'but only a little bit — aesthetes and drunkenness don't match...'

'Granddad's never drunk,' I said, just to be on the safe side as Gran might be wrong, but then we heard him swearing again. He was saying terrible things and screaming for my gran, and then we went quite quiet and Gran put her arm around me. 'Don't be scared,' she whispered, but I could tell she was frightened, and then Granddad got his key in the lock and stumbled into the hall.

Next morning I drag myself into the bathroom. My head feels awful, and when I feel around underneath my hair with one hand I find a big round bump. I lock the door and bend over the washbasin so I can run cold water over the back of my head. Mum's still in bed and Anne's out jogging. She's been obsessed with fitness for a while now – so she doesn't put on weight, she says. If you ask me it's more like so the boys round here have something to look at. But she gets really mad if you say that. Lizzy says that's a sign that I'm right. Lizzy knows all about that kind of thing. Anyway, Anne goes jogging round the block nearly every morning, wearing black hot pants and tight T-shirts, and by the time she gets back she's so red in the face you can't see a single freckle any more, and when I tease her about it she says, 'Well, you don't have to worry about your figure do you, you're such a beanpole you never put on weight.' What she means is that I've got no breasts and no bum, and that makes me pretty much the least feminine person on earth in her book.

I wrap a towel round my soaking wet hair and take off my nightie. Anne's right I suppose; I turn around and look at my tiny bum in the mirror. The front of me's not much better – you can see my hip bones quite clearly and my shoulders are a bit bony too. And then my breasts, or what's supposed to be breasts one day. Lizzy and I quite often compare our chests. We go in Lizzy's bathroom and Lizzy says: 'Anything to report on the boob front?' We giggle and pull our T-shirts up over our heads. Then we pretend to interview our breasts, so I'll say in the voice of my right breast: 'Well I could use a bit of reinforcement,' and Lizzy says: 'I'd say so too, young lady.' Lizzy's the only person in the world who's allowed to make fun of my breasts, and that's because she hasn't got much in that department either so we're more or less in the same boat. We often console each other by saying that big boobs wouldn't suit us anyway, but if we're really honest with each other we would actually like big ones, and we even envy Anne a tiny bit.

But whoa – looking in the mirror today there's a tiny change, only teeny-tiny, but still. It looks like there's more under my nipples, and if I press them with my fingers it hurts, I mean my breasts hurt, and Lizzy's mother says when your breasts start to hurt it means they're growing. I lean right up to the mirror to get a better look, and then I give my reflection a big grin. There's no doubt about it they're growing. Lizzy'll be amazed when I tell her! I'm really excited all of a sudden, as if something big was going to happen in my life; I'm actually certain something big's going to happen, today, right now, as soon as I go out of the house. I put on a black top and my best jeans. They're really faded and threadbare and unfortunately a bit too short; Mum doesn't like them much, she says I look scruffy in them. But Mum's still asleep so she won't see me leaving the house. I grab the basket of Tupperware boxes and the keys to my bike.

Screwy is standing at the garden gate. Screwy and Anne. I gasp for breath and stop stockstill on the steps. They're having a great laugh. Anne's wearing a cropped top, her jogging gear, and she's got her hands on her hips. She's laughing and flinging her head back and shaking her hair, which shines in the sun like gold. Gross. Screwy's resting one arm on our garden wall, laughing too; I can see his crooked nose in profile. The two of them are so busy they don't even notice me. Shocked for a second, I freeze on the steps, long enough to brand their image onto my brain. Anne and Screwy. Screwy and Anne.

Then I feel my way cautiously back into the hall, close the door and lean my back against it. My heart is thumping, knocking against my throat like crazy.

What an idiot, I think. He was just messing me about and it's really Anne he's into, like all the boys. He's hanging out with me to get to know my sister. Lizzy was so right, we shouldn't have anything to do with those boys from the estate, it echoes in my mind. *Especially not that Screwy…*

I hear Anne laughing, it sounds put on like she laughs when she wants to impress someone. I know that laugh – last year Lizzy and I caught Anne in Smoker's Corner. That's a hidden corner near our school where secret couples go and people who want to smoke, because smoking and secret couples are banned at school. We walked along the track behind school, it winds through dense bushes and it's covered in cigarette ends, chocolate wrappers, beer cans, and sometimes you can even find used condoms. We were walking along there because Lizzy had decided we ought to have a go at smoking; she'd got hold of two cigarettes, nicked out of her mum's packet, and hidden them in her jacket.

It was a windy day with rain on the air, and I was just doubting we'd even get the cigarettes lit when the wind blew the sound of laughter over to us. Lizzy stopped so suddenly we bumped into each other. We stood still and there was that laugh again. As we crept nearer we could see Anne through the bushes, sitting on a boy's lap, and the boy was sitting on the ventilation shaft that everyone used as a seat, everyone who wanted to smoke or snog there.

'I don't believe it,' I whispered.

For a while we watched Anne getting off with the boy, and then we made our way back. Somehow we'd forgotten all about the cigarettes.

Now I'm leaning against the door with Anne's laughter sounding in my ears. So that's the way it is, Mr Screwy, I think, congratulating myself on my own stupidity. It's obvious he'd rather be standing around flirting with Anne than with me.

Even though my knees feel like rubber I manage to sprint through the house with my basket of Tupperware and vanish out of the back door. Let them, I think as I climb over the garden fence. Of course I get stuck and tear a hole in the bum of my favourite jeans. The two of them can just go to hell!

I get to Granddad's building pretty exhausted. Stupidly enough I couldn't take my bike, it's still chained to the railings outside our house where Screwy and Anne are flirting. I've got a blister on one heel; strappy sandals aren't suitable for long walks. I sit down on a bench at the edge of the little play area, kick off my sandals and stare straight ahead. The horse chestnuts rustle in the wind above me, their scent filling the little back yard. I stare at the place where the dragon slide used to be. All that's left is stamped-down brown earth, a couple of sand toys and a plastic digger that probably belonged to one of Mrs Bitschek's kids.

As I sit there like that I find myself trying to turn the pages of the photo album in my mind. The one with all the blind spots. Before my eyes, the dragon slide appears and I see myself climbing through its brightly coloured, contorted body; I see my gran: She's small and wearing a dark-blue skirt down to her calves and a pale blouse. She's got pearl earrings in her wrinkly earlobes. I try to turn the page but I can't. There's only ever this picture and nothing else. Not me walking up the stairs or sitting in the living room, and I think to myself, what on earth was I doing all that time?

A gust of wind blows through the horse chestnut trees and rains a shower of white blossoms down on me, onto my head, my legs, my arms, into the basket next to me on the bench. Mum's made stew, which looks pretty disgusting in the Tupperware boxes; I can't look.

Bratko wanders past, jumping up onto one of the big bins with an elegant leap and crouching on the very edge so that there's barely room for his paws.

He's eyeing the birds but I bet he's too fat to catch anything. Where Bratko is, Mrs Bitschek can't be far away, and there you go, a minute later she comes strolling across the yard to me. She sits down next to me on the bench.

'Nice and quiet,' she says, and I nod. Her children are at school and nursery this morning, and the baby's asleep upstairs. Another gust of wind blusters the toys around and blows Mrs Bitschek's polka-dot skirt out like a balloon.

'Mrs Bitschek,' I say, 'can you remember your childhood?'

Mrs Bitschek gives me a sideways searching look.

'Yes, of course,' she says then.

We watch the toys getting blown across the patch of sand. Mrs Bitschek has to hold her skirt down with both hands so no one can see her underwear.

'And you?' she says. 'What about your childhood?'

She says it as if I was grown up, as if we were talking woman to woman; it feels good. It's never like that with Mum. She and Anne treat me like a little kid, so I usually don't even want to talk to them. They roll their eyes behind my back and give each other secret looks, and sometimes Anne says I'll get over puberty one day, as if my age was a terrible disease, as if I was a leper or something. Lizzy says I shouldn't take any notice, Anne's just a stupid cow, and she's right there; whenever I think of Anne I get really mad with her. It's best not to think about her at all or else I might burst, she makes me so angry.

'I can't remember at all,' I say, not taking my eyes off the toys, and before I realise what I'm doing I'm telling her the thing about the photo album with the blind spots, and that I often try and turn the page but I can't. As I'm telling her I realise how often I really think of the photo album. A lot, since Granddad kissed me – every day actually. I don't tell Mrs Bitschek about that of course, I'm scared she'd react the same way as Paul and Dad. I've sworn to never mention it to anyone else, because all grown-ups probably think the same thing, and maybe Granddad was right when he said the others would think there's something wrong with me. I'm starting to feel like that myself – that something's wrong with me.

Mrs Bitschek listens to me and then she doesn't say anything for a long time, until I start to think she might have fallen asleep next to me or she doesn't want to talk about blind spots.

Then she says: 'Your granddad's looking, he stands whole time behind curtain and looks.'

I feel that familiar tingling in my neck and don't dare to turn round.

'Your granddad has bad spirit,' Mrs Bitschek says quietly, and the tingling in my neck gets stronger because it's really spooky to have a granddad with a bad spirit.

Bratko jumps off the bin and wanders over to us. His fur is all ruffled by the wind, standing up in all directions whichever way the wind blows it.

He presses up against my legs and then jumps onto Mrs Bitschek's lap, purring.

'Like Bratko?' I ask.

Mrs Bitschek shakes her head and strokes Bratko's back. He arches his back and closes his eyes.

'No,' she says, 'Bratko is poor devil, can't help being like nature made him, but your granddad has spirit.'

She taps her head so I know what she means. She means he's got something up there, at least more than Bratko.

'He can choose good or bad, and he chooses bad.'

She carries on stroking Bratko's back until he waves his tail in protest and heads off.

The thoughts are whirling around in my mind. One of the blind spots is suddenly full of colour, luminous colour, and there's no blurring now. I see the carpet, the red one with the black square patterns, and my gran's legs, I see the varicose veins winding in knots around her legs, and her tan-coloured tights. She's standing in front of me stroking my head, and her voice sounds as if she'd just been crying. That was my seventh birthday, I think. Right, that was the morning of my seventh birthday, and if I raised my head I'd see a cake with seven pink candles on the table. I've just come out of the bathroom. Granddad wrapped me in a bathrobe and then went out. The bathrobe is scratchy, it's made of pale-blue towelling; I can't stand this bathrobe.

'Granddad can't help it,' Gran said.

And that was a lie.

We hear children shouting and screaming, Mrs Bitschek's children coming home for lunch. They run into the back yard and throw themselves at Mrs Bitschek; she laughs and hugs them, talking to them in Polish, which I don't understand of course. She gets up and herds them into the house.

'Shall I?' she asks, pointing at the basket, but I shake my head.

Then I'm alone, alone outside the house where my memory got holes in it, alone outside the house where everything began.

Friday

Granddad stumbled into the hall and Gran pressed me firmly against her body with one arm. Her head-scarf had slipped and I could see her bare head; it was very pale pink with slight wrinkles and soft white down where her hair was beginning to grow back sparsely. From outside, crashing noises came through to us – Granddad trying to hang his jacket on the coat-stand and knocking it over, slipping his shoes off and tripping on the carpet in his bare feet.

'Shhh...' said my gran and rocked me in her arms. 'Shhh...nothing's going to happen.'

I crept onto her lap, rolling myself up as small as I could and pressing my hands to my ears. But I could still hear every word. He hammered his fists against the door, every vibration making us jump. 'Hilda!' he shouted, that was my gran's name, 'Send her out, send my Malvina out!'

He shouted it over and over as Gran and I clung to each other, and I said I wouldn't go out there and I was really scared, and Gran said, 'You have to be brave, you have to be very brave now.'

And after a while Gran sent me out. She didn't look at me as she did it, just opened the door a crack and pushed me through, and Granddad caught me, lifted me up and carried me into the living room.

'My little Malvina,' he kept saying, 'my little Malvina.'

I didn't say anything at all, I had my eyes shut, I smelled alcohol and men's sweat, I felt swathes of light falling across my face and then the velvety cover of the sofa he laid me down on. I thought something terrible was going to happen because he'd been so angry before, when he noticed Gran had locked us into the kitchen, but actually nothing happened. He pressed me to his body, pressed my face into his neck and mumbled confused nonsense, that he loved me and I shouldn't be afraid of him. He'd never do anything to harm me, he said, he couldn't do that, he loved me so much, and he just wanted to hold me in his arms, nothing else.

After a while he fell asleep and his head tipped to one side; a little later I heard Gran opening the kitchen door quietly, and I climbed over Granddad's long legs, carefully so I didn't wake him up, and crept out to Gran in the hall. She was crying and she took my hand.

We waited downstairs for Dad to pick me up. We didn't talk to each other; I climbed on the dragon slide, right to the top so that Gran couldn't see my face and because I felt normal on the slide. A perfectly normal day. Nothing alarming had happened, nothing bad, everything was just the way it always was.

The worst thing about breakfast is Anne. She's sitting in her jogging gear with her legs up on the chair, jigging her feet in time to the music on the radio. Mum's poking around in her muesli with a long-suffering look on her face and Dad's reading the paper; that always annoys Mum because his paper takes up half the table every time, but Dad says she shouldn't get so het up, it's not good for her migraines and her bowl doesn't take up more than two square inches of space anyway.

I throw evil glances at Anne across the breakfast table, but she doesn't even notice – she's much too preoccupied with herself. As she nibbles on half a slice of toast she inspects the tips of her hair for split ends. Anne is constantly worrying about her hair, she uses a thousand different treatments to protect it from environmental damage. Lizzy and I think that's pretty dumb. We cut our hair ourselves, I cut Lizzy's and Lizzy cuts mine, and that saves us loads of money that we can spend on ice creams.

My hands are on the table next to my plate; I can't eat, every single bite would get stuck in my throat. I wish I could scream at Anne to keep her dirty paws off Screwy, and then I'd shout out that I've turned the pages of the album, yes I have, yesterday I turned a page for the first time, and I'm going to turn more pages. I have a funny feeling it's going to be easy to find the right pages and fill the blind spots with colour. It made me restless and jittery, worked up because I know there's something sleeping inside me, it has been for a long time, and now it's ready to wake up, it's turning over reluctantly, yawning and stretching, but soon it's going to open its eyes, and I'll look through those eyes. I'm very close. My hands tingle and my neck too, and there's a numb feeling in my chest as if my heart had moved out.

'I'm not going round to Granddad's any more,' I say, looking down at my empty plate and my restless hands. My words surprise me – I didn't plan them, they just came crashing out of me, like a badly healed wound sometimes opens up again. I feel their eyes resting on me, then Mum gets up and puts her bowl in the dishwasher, making incredibly slow movements that I can see out of the corner of my eye. When she's done she leans against the dresser and looks out of the window. There's one of her bird houses out there. The radio blares, Dad rustles the pages of his newspaper and Anne devotes all her attention to her split ends.

'I'm not going any more,' I repeat; I get the feeling they must not have heard me for some reason. Silence reigns once again, and Anne tips backwards on her chair to the radio on the kitchen shelf, turns it up and hums along to the tune.

'What's all this nonsense about?' Dad says at last, putting his newspaper down on the table. 'Granddad's always very happy when you visit him. He's been lonely since Gran died. I thought my children had educated hearts.'

He says that thing about educated hearts quite a lot – such and such a person doesn't have an educated heart, that's what it comes down to. He despises people whose hearts aren't educated, and now he thinks mine isn't, so he despises me. He bends down to me; he has steely-blue eyes and he looks into mine as if he could see my heart, my uneducated little heart that's cowering in a corner in fear.

'Do you even know what an educated heart is?' he asks.

I shake my head; my heart probably isn't even there any more, just a numb space somewhere in the middle of my body.

'An educated heart means having sympathy for other people. And not letting people down just because they're old and sick.'

Everything is muddled up in my head; what Dad says sounds right, it just doesn't feel right, there's a catch somewhere, I know there is, there's something Dad's not saying.

Anne starts clearing the table, squeezing past me and nudging me in the side.

'Listen and learn, kid,' she says. It sounds deliberately laid-back, as if it was all none of her business.

'Letting an old person down is a rotten thing to

do,' says Dad, and my insides lurch; I leap up from my chair.

'No,' I say, 'no, no, no!'

I can't stop any more, as if a record had got stuck in my head, and I get louder and louder, louder than the radio, louder than the dishwasher that Anne's just turned on.

'No!' I shout.

'That's not true! That's not true at all!' I shout.

Mum puts her hands over her ears and runs out of the room, pale faced, her mouth a thin line pressed together. I hear her bedroom door slam. She'll lock herself in there and won't come out for hours. It's my fault.

Dad jumps up; for a moment it looks as if he's going to run after her but then he stays put, right in front of me. He's livid, the artery in his neck is pulsing. Anne gets out of the kitchen quick, leaving me alone with Dad.

'She really did get a blow to the head,' she says, rolling her eyes as she leaves. She means the thing with the telephone table, and she means I'm not quite right in the brain.

Thoughts shoot through my head, I think he'll hit me. I pull my head back, duck down on my chair. Dad's still standing in front of me, the slam of Mum's bedroom door still echoing in my ears.

'Right,' he says with restraint. 'So it's not true, is it? You're accusing me of lying?'

I duck down even further and don't answer. The

storm is brewing above my head, Dad's storm. I can't
help thinking about what Screwy said, that he nearly
hit that boy in his class, and I can't help thinking of
the times when he's been angry with me, so angry he
shouted, he can shout very loudly, so loudly you wish
you could crawl under the table, and I can't help
thinking of the times he's hit me. I don't think I'd
dare to hit back, not even on the spur of the moment
like Screwy said.

'So,' he insists, 'what are you trying to say?'

'Nothing,' I say quietly, and suddenly it feels like
that's true, I wasn't trying to say anything, it's
nobody's business. I might as well lock up the photo
album, all this stuff inside me, bury it, leave it
behind sealed with a padlock. It's none of their
business, it's nobody's business, it's not even my own
business.

'That's all right then,' says Dad. 'That's all right
then.'

He sits back down at the table and picks up his
paper, and me – I pick up my basket. Granddad's
waiting.

I hope I never see Screwy again. I'm so ashamed I fell
for his stupid games. Thinking about him telling his
friends makes my blood boil with horror. I can imagine every word he says, I can even imagine what his
face looks like as he says it. He'll light a cigarette and
look around at them with a superior expression. *I
gave that kid from the villa the run-around in the Easter*

holidays, he'll say. *She was so dumb she didn't even notice.* And his mates will wet themselves laughing. What a gruesome scene. I'm going to have to tell Lizzy about it, for better or worse, and she's not exactly going to be pleased. She'll want revenge.

Anne waylays me by the front door.

'Let me out,' I say. 'I'll kick you in the shin if you don't let me out.'

She raises her eyebrows and grins.

'Ouch!' she says in a falsetto voice, 'I'm really scared now.'

She folds her arms in front of her chest.

'Listen you, you can save the rebellious teenager show,' she says, leaning her back against the door.

I don't know what she wants from me. I get the feeling everyone just wants to let out their anger on me. I have to take the rap for everything, I have to put up with Mum's migraines and Dad's frustration, and now Anne as well. I can't stand the sight of her black owl's eyes and her red-painted mouth.

With all my strength and without even thinking, I kick her in the shin. I don't know where I get the strength from, but I did warn her. Anne screeches and hops around the hall.

'You're not right in the head,' she roars, and I run past her out of the door.

'Then I won't tell you,' she shouts, 'you moody cow!'

'I don't care anyway!' I shout back. 'I don't care any more what you lot want from me.'

I unlock my bike with jittery fingers. I've no idea why I'm shaking like this, I'm not scared of my sister but I feel as if an abyss was opening up underneath me. From far off, I hear Anne shouting and screaming, saying she hates me and she'll get a bruise on her leg and I only ever make trouble. I'm a useless brat who only ever makes trouble.

'And you'll never find out what that boy said,' she shouts, 'Never!'

I don't notice the note clamped under my luggage carrier until I lock my bike again in Granddad's back yard. It's from Screwy – I know that even before I read it. His handwriting's pretty spidery and messy and the paper is crumpled, probably because he had it in his pocket. I frown and unfold the note.

Where were you yesterday? it says, *I looked for you. See you at the villa this afternoon?*

I crumple up the paper and throw it in the glass-recycling bin as I pass it. Pull the other one – it's got bells on it.

I carry on, my steps firm, up the stairs, past Mrs Bitschek's front door; I can smell pancakes, the TV is on and the baby's screaming. And I can hear Mrs Bitschek singing.

Granddad opens the door for me. 'Malvina, my little Malvina,' he says, hugging me tight.

We listen to records, just like in the old days – the old days when Gran was here. Time blurs, and I'm little again, very little, so small I can roll myself up on

Granddad's lap. I don't understand the record, it's in German, but I know it's Nietzsche, Granddad told me that. Nietzsche's another one of those philosophers; he said God is dead. Maybe he's right, I think as I roll myself up next to Granddad; God wouldn't let something like this happen. God would put everything right. Granddad strokes my hair and my neck, now and then the record jumps, it makes a funny crackling sound and the speaker pauses, a tiny pause to catch his breath. I can't catch my breath. I lie there and listen. I wait for it to be over. Granddad pulls me up so that my head's on his lap, nothing else, he strokes me, pushing his hand under my T-shirt and down my back. I close my eyes and see the clouds floating by. My body's not important, not important at all, I'm lifeless, only my thoughts fly away, that's all that counts; you can't hold down thoughts. I can go wherever I want.

'My little woman,' says Granddad.

He feels his way on, feels for my breasts, it doesn't matter, it doesn't matter at all, he can do whatever he wants as long as he doesn't touch my thoughts.

'Just like the old days,' he says. 'Do you remember?'

Then I hold my ears closed, I press my hands to my ears, I hum the tune from the radio this morning, I don't know anything, I can't remember, and I won't turn any more pages in the album. Anything, just not that, that's what comes into my mind now, and this thought drives the clouds out of my head like an icy draft sweeping through the room and whirling up the pages of a book, my book. A couple of photos fall out, slip through my fingers, and horror creeps across my body.

'We were so happy together, the three of us, you, Gran and me. Now there's just the two of us.' He takes my hands off my ears so that I can hear every word.

'We were so happy together.'

I hear myself breathing, the record rotates, the speaker reads on and on in his monotonous singsong voice, and Granddad kisses my neck, my shoulders, not noticing me turning to ice under his kisses.

'We can be happy again like that,' he says, and his voice sounds agitated, breathless.

'We just have to take care that no one finds out, they'd take you away, do you understand, Malvina, they'd tear us apart, they'd say you're not right. They'd judge you.'

His voice drones in my ears. *Take you away,* it echoes, *judge you, you're not right, happy again like the old days, the two of us.*

'Do you remember how nice it was?' says Granddad.

I shake my head and he laughs, he thinks I'm joking; he gives me a slight shake.

'Don't be silly, Malvina,' he says with a laugh, 'you must remember.'

Someone knocks at the door from outside. Granddad hesitates, then he gets up and marches to the door, looking angry, his back stiff and straight. He opens the door.

'What do you want?' he says in a harsh tone of voice.

Mrs Bitschek gives a quiet, friendly answer, she says I have to help her carry the pram downstairs, she says please, and that it's too heavy for her, she's got a bad back. She repeats the words *bad back* a few times to make sure Granddad understands her. I smooth out my T-shirt.

'The record's finished anyway,' I tell Granddad.

He's very angry but he has to let me go. We carry the pram down the stairs, I say a hasty goodbye and Mrs Bitschek tells me to come and visit her, maybe tomorrow. I say maybe, avoiding her eyes.

saturday

The boys weren't fooled for long by Lizzy's trick last summer. If we thought they'd be put off by an imaginary gang leader, we had another think coming.

For a couple of days they slunk around the villa, keeping an eye out for us and our leader. Lizzy and I made sure we got to the villa as early as possible, earlier than the boys, so that they didn't see just the two of us going in. It turned out Lizzy's trick was pretty stupid. We ended up sitting around inside all day, waiting for the boys to turn up. The heat was unbearable, especially in the attic, and we got bored to death with all the waiting. Then one day when there'd been no sign of them by the early afternoon we lost our patience. We'd climbed up into the beams to keep watch on the path to the villa, and Lizzy had got badly sunburned on her shoulders.

'I've had it up to here,' she moaned, plucking at her vest that was rubbing uncomfortably against her burned shoulders.

'What d'you reckon, they're not coming any more, are they? They want to let us fry up here,' said Lizzy. 'I bet they've gone for a nice swim while we're up here.'

We balanced our way back along the beams and dropped down onto my pile of cushions on the mattress; you have to have a good aim to do that and be brave enough to jump. If you don't aim right you can do yourself a lot of harm. Once I sprained my ankle doing it, but I still keep on jumping. I'm not a coward, am I? Lizzy dropped down first; the feathers came flying out of the cushions, like snowflakes in the middle of summer. Before I jumped I took one last look over my shoulder towards the estate, but I swear there was no one there, at least no boys on bikes. I plopped down and wished the feathers really were snowflakes, it was so hot.

'We could go swimming too,' I suggested. That was what I really wanted to do, even more than getting in a fight with the boys.

Seeing as Lizzy really wanted a swim too, we were in a bit of a dilemma. Go swimming and abandon the villa, or fry slowly up here. We spent a while weighing up our options but we couldn't really make a decision – until Lizzy had an idea that saved the day.

There was an old wooden water butt behind the villa, which the rain from the gutters flowed into, and it'd be a huge laugh to get into it, Lizzy said. It wouldn't be as good as in our old frog pond of course, but it was worth a try. So we ran out into the garden, the sun burning down on us through the leaves of the fruit trees. Soon the cherries would be ripe and after that the apples and the plums, and when the plums are ripe the summer's over.

We slipped out of our shorts and vests – that summer we thought it was really cool to wear ribbed men's vests – and hung them over the lowest branch of an apple tree only a few steps away from the water barrel. The water in the butt was pretty murky; it was brown and smelled brackish and was absolutely covered in tiny pale-green duckweed leaves. You couldn't possibly see the bottom of the barrel but we decided that only made it more exciting. It was almost like a dare to get into the butt. First we stabbed about in the barrel with a stick, swirling up the duckweed – we didn't want to tread on a dead bird lying around somewhere on the bottom, and I said we should at least leave our shoes on, just in case we'd overlooked something disgusting, and Lizzy agreed; she didn't want to run that risk either.

'Yuck,' she giggled. 'Maybe we'll put our toes in Evil Frederick's nostrils!'

That was such a disgusting idea that we both pulled back our legs quickly, even though they were already in the water at that point.

'Rubbish,' I said, 'that means Evil Frederick must have had his head chopped off.'

'His wife did it, I bet she'd had enough of him,' said Lizzy, 'what with the way he looked.'

We stabbed about with the stick again just in case, and when we didn't find any nostrils or anything like that we climbed over the edge and into the butt.

I dream of running along dark passageways, of my gran with tubes attached to her arms, with electrodes attached to her wrinkly chest; she stretches her hands out for me, and I run and run and run. I wake up in the morning drenched in sweat, at the first light that falls into my room, and then I jump out of bed and take a shower. I have to turn the water up very hot to get rid of the dream. I don't look at myself in the mirror any more, not naked – my own body is a traitor. As long as I've taken my shower and keep moving there's no problem. I just mustn't stop moving, mustn't start thinking.

The other problem is Screwy. Screwy's getting on my nerves. I tell him so too when I catch him lying in wait for me in Granddad's back yard, hiding behind the glass-recycling bin, but I spot him before he spots me – I can smell him. He's smoking again and the smoke gets up my nose. Screwy gets the shock of his life when I talk to him. Serves him right; I didn't ask him to follow me around all day long, did I?

'Jesus,' he says, 'don't creep up on me like that!'

It's warmer today than the last few days. Soon it'll be summer, soon we'll be able to go swimming and go barefoot again. Screwy's wearing short, frayed jeans, they look sort of funny on him because he's got bandy legs. But I still pull an angry face so he knows right away that I don't feel like making small talk.

'I'll do what I like, and anyway I can't stand you spying on me. It's really annoying,' I tell him.

Screwy grins, puts out his cigarette on his shoe and throws it in the bin. He obviously doesn't care if he sets fire to the bin; I know I wouldn't be able to relax for a minute if I did that.

'What about the villa?' he says. 'Shall we go over there?'

He doesn't seem to be wondering why I stood him up yesterday, and he's obviously not feeling guilty about Anne. Lizzy would say it just goes to show how hard-boiled the boys from the estate are, they'd rob their own grandmothers and then laugh in your face. At any rate I don't intend to let Screwy mess me around any more. Let him spend his holidays with other people. Like Anne for one – she'd probably love him to put his arm round her shoulders, and she wouldn't get moody either.

'No time,' I say roughly.

'I thought it was the Easter holidays,' he says, shoving his hands in his pockets. He always does that when he's unsure of himself.

'I have to look after my granddad,' I say.

If you ask me it's always best to stay very close to the truth. The closer the better. You almost never get caught out with that kind of lie because it would be much too simple.

'Right,' says Screwy. 'That's a lie.'

My face goes a fiery shade of red and Screwy watches with smug satisfaction.

'He's sick,' I say, going even redder.

Screwy shakes his head.

'Let me tell you something,' he says. 'I've been standing here for about the last hour and a half. I know your granddad, you can't miss him because he's tall and he wears an eye-patch. About forty-five minutes ago the guy walked past me. He came from that direction and he was carrying a sandwich and a drink. He hassled me, told me not to hang round here like a lout, and I told him to bugger off and leave me alone. What I'm trying to say is, the guy's not sick and he's not starving to death, so I don't understand why you have to look after him in your Easter holidays.'

'You told him to bugger off?' I say, amazed.

'Yeah,' says Screwy, 'I can hang around wherever I want, and anyway I was pretty sure you'd turn up sooner or later.'

The craziest things spool through my head. Why Screwy's waiting for me here when he was flirting with Anne. Why he's watching my granddad and how he dares to tell my granddad to bugger off. I wouldn't have the guts. Never! I'd be much too scared that Granddad would lose his temper and shout at me like he used to shout at Gran so often.

'So are you coming with me then?' says Screwy. 'I can take him his basket, I can go up and say, here you are, this is from your granddaughter and now I'm

118

going to make sure she doesn't waste her time hanging round with you any more.'

Screwy reaches out his hand for the basket and I take a step backwards.

'You can't do that,' I say, thinking like crazy what to tell Screwy. He and Granddad mustn't come face to face a second time. Screwy mustn't turn up here at all, ever again. Granddad will go completely mad if he looks out of the window and spots us down here. It'd be even worse if Screwy found out anything about Granddad. If he found out what I'm keeping locked up in my heart. He'd loathe me, he'd hate me, he'd tell his friends and they'd tell Lizzy. Maybe Lizzy would hate me too and find a new best friend.

'You mustn't come here any more,' I say, feeling the world start to spin around me again. Like two days ago in Granddad's living room. The ground sways under my feet and I see black spots on Screwy's face, getting bigger and bigger, so big there's not much left of Screwy's face.

Actually, I think to myself, this fainting thing's not that bad. I could faint and never wake up again, or I could faint and be taken to hospital, I could spend a couple of years under a blanket in hospital until I'm grown up and Granddad's dead and everything comes right by itself.

Before I tip over again Screwy pulls me behind the bin into a laburnum bush, and I fall on my bottom.

'You'd better put your head between your knees,' he says.

I put my head between my knees and hope the spinning will stop.

'That'll be from your concussion,' he says. 'You should've gone to the doctor's.'

'I'm fine,' I say.

'I can see that,' says Screwy. 'You're even paler than the other day, you look really crap to be honest.'

Behind us, Bratko creeps through the bushes. There's a cracking and rustling sound and Bratko gives a pitiful *meow* as if he was terribly upset about something, but he's probably just hungry. Mrs Bitschek's put him on a diet and since then he's been grumpier than ever. She said he'd die of a fatty heart if he doesn't lose weight.

I keep my head between my knees and don't answer. I don't owe Screwy an explanation, do I? I don't even want to talk to him, all I want is for him to leave me alone, for him to get out of here and stop asking questions. He can flirt with Anne all he likes, then he'll have something to do and he can't stick his nose in my business.

'Hey, are you still alive?' he says, giving me a cautious nudge.

I shake my head and feel tears welling up in my eyes. I try to blink them away but it won't work properly. Oh great, now I can stay here until I start gathering moss. I don't want him to see me blubbing – the only person who's allowed to see me cry is Lizzy and nobody else. My gran used to be allowed too, but since she's been dead I haven't cried much at all.

'Just leave me alone,' I say, pressing my face into my knees. 'I'm absolutely fine, d'you get it, I just want to be left alone, that's all. You can hang out with Anne, you get on really well with her, don't you?'

This time Screwy doesn't say anything. All I can hear is his breathing. Bratko rolls in the dirt in front of us, probably as revenge on Mrs Bitschek, that'd be just like him.

'My granddad doesn't like strangers, he's really funny like that,' I say.

I can hear my blood rushing in my ears. If you don't watch out, it whispers, he'll find out everything, if you start blubbing he won't stop asking questions. He'll stay sitting next to you here until you've told him everything, everything you know, everything you remember, and then, what then? Then he'll run off and tell everyone, he won't be able to keep his mouth shut.

'You're taking the mickey,' says Screwy. 'What do I want with your sister? And I don't care about your granddad, I want to go to the villa with you, not with him. You're talking crap. Shall I tell you what I think?'

My heart skips a beat with shock. Here it comes now, he's going to say it now, I think. He's going to say I'm not normal and he knows all about Granddad, he'll say all these unsayable things and throw them in my face. It'll be no use holding my ears closed, he'll bring everything to light, right here in a laburnum bush behind the glass-recycling bin.

'You might as well just tell me if you don't like me,' he says, 'because of last summer.'

The chaos of thoughts in my mind is getting worse and worse, I can't listen any more; all I want is to be alone. Alone and in peace. What does he want from me? I don't understand how he can start with last summer.

'You're inventing all these excuses because you really can't stand me. But I didn't think you were such a coward, I thought you'd dare anything, and now you're lying and lying and lying. Maybe I don't go to a good school like you do but that doesn't make me stupid,' he says. 'You could at least admit you don't like me.'

I bite my tongue, stubborn. He hasn't got it at all. Relief floods over me in waves. He doesn't know, he hasn't got a clue.

'I'm not going until you tell me,' says Screwy. 'We were pretty mean to each other last year but that's a long time ago now, I'm not angry with you any more about . . .'

He breaks off and stops talking.

'Just leave me alone,' I say.

I know my voice sounds pressed, and if Screwy can add two and two together he's sure to notice I'm going to burst out crying as soon as he leaves. He gets up and stops in front of me, wavering slightly; his trainers are right in my line of vision. His trainers with two different coloured laces, his wiry, crooked calves, his frayed jeans. I'm scared he's going to stand there for ever, but then his bandy legs move off, the laburnum folding together behind them.

'That's that then,' I say quietly to Bratko. 'That's got rid of him.'

The cat blinks at me, then shakes his dusty coat, and I start to cry.

Sunday

We were happy. I started going to piano lessons every Friday. I took my time on the way back, but all I actually had to do was cross the road and there were Gran and Granddad. Gran's hair grew back, she didn't have to wear a headscarf any more, and Granddad said that was all down to me. The colour came back to her cheeks but her eyes looked past me, empty. We didn't sit on the kitchen floor together and talk any more, and her touch was wooden. When I came over from my piano lesson she opened the door. There was vanilla ice cream on the table in the living room, slowly melting in its glass bowl. I stirred it around with my spoon until it turned to mush, and Gran said: 'Eat up before he comes.'

When he came home I hid behind the sofa. He thought it was a game, a game I liked to play. For my sake he pretended not to find me. He searched the flat, room by room, even though he knew perfectly well I was crouching behind the sofa. There was no other hiding place, I always waited behind the sofa. He walked through the flat.

'Where's my little Malvina?' he said. 'Where is she?'

He started in the hall, then he rattled around in the kitchen, looking in the cupboards, between the saucepans, in the wardrobe in the bedroom, behind the curtains, taking his time but never long enough; he always found me long before anyone came to pick me up. Dad or Paul or Anne. Mum never came anyway, and the others always came too late.

Once he'd looked in every room, he came into the living room. I could see his brown slippers, his feet shuffling across the carpet in them. First he looked behind the armchair, but I wasn't there. He opened the window, 'Has my little Malvina flown away?' he said. Then he knelt down in front of the sofa, slowly because his knees hurt, his joints made funny noises and he sighed a little so that I noticed how much of an effort he was going to on my account. He pushed his head into the gap behind the sofa; it was dark and dusty there because Gran couldn't bend over to do the cleaning any more, she called the fluffy round balls that flew around under the furniture dust bunnies. He waited for his eye to adjust to the darkness.

'Ah, I can see something,' he said. 'What can it be? A little Malvina, perhaps.'

That was the end of the game, and I climbed over the back of the sofa, leaving little Malvina behind back there. She stayed motionless among the dust bunnies, letting time run backwards. She sat on the kitchen floor with her gran and told stories and hung upside-down on the dragon slide, laughing.

The other Malvina climbed over the back of the sofa and followed her granddad into the bathroom, the little green-tiled room that always smelled of Ajax and bubble bath. He heated up the boiler, which took a little while, and the other Malvina stood on the bathmat, watching the gas flame inside the boiler flitting about and the water splashing into the bathtub a little later. The bubble bath foamed up and Granddad laughed.

'Bubbles make you beautiful,' he always said, pouring more and more of the honey-brown, syrupy bubble bath into the tub. I couldn't stand the bubble bath, the smell sent waves of nausea rolling through my stomach. It smelled of old men's perfume, the way men often smell at church on Sunday, when they kneel in the pew and you can see their thin strands of hair from behind. I hated that smell. I hated the bath, I hated the fact that I never got a word out, never dared to say anything. I hated being so scared of him, hated taking my clothes off without a word, folding them up on the washing machine and getting into the bath with him. In the bath I couldn't see what he was doing, I could only feel his bony body under the mountains of foam. He liked the foam, it made him feel safe. His hands flashed to and fro in the water like smooth, nimble fish. The fish pulled me onto his lap; it made him happy when I sat on his lap, leaning my back on his chest.

'When I'm happy Gran's happy too,' he said. 'You're making your gran very, very happy.'

We stayed in the bath like that for a long time, until there was no foam left, then he wrapped me in the blue bathrobe and sent me out. By the time my dad and my brother and sister came I was dry and dressed. Gran blow-dried my hair. She dried it in the kitchen, so hot that it hurt the back of my neck, but I didn't say a word. I clenched my teeth. I wanted Gran to be happy, and I didn't want the cancer to eat her up from inside. That was all that counted.

This is the first Sunday I haven't waited for Paul. My spot on the garden wall is empty. I watch the road from the window. I can see myself sitting there, my hair glinting in the sun – it even looks a bit red in the sunshine. I have to sit on my hands or my bum will get cold from the wall; I can feel the rough bricks under my skin.

Paul's bright-yellow Smart car turns onto our street. Any minute now he'll pick me up and whirl me around. 'You're not eating enough,' he'll say, putting his big hands round my wrists.

'What are you moping around here for?' says Anne.

She's laying the table for lunch. She's still angry about the bruises on her shin, and she clatters extra loudly with the plates. I lose myself outside; it feels strange, I vanish somewhere and my empty shell stays behind at the window, leaning on the windowsill.

'Hey,' says Anne, 'give me a hand instead.'

Paul parks his Smart car by the garden gate. He looks like he's in a good mood, not at all like he's wondering where I am. He doesn't even notice I'm not there. He springs up the garden path – he always runs like that, like someone training for a marathon, someone really fit. I turn away from the window. They'll all be here in a minute. I plunge into my empty shell, it gives you a headache and makes your heart race, and I wonder if it sometimes happens that you can't find your way back to your shell. Maybe the others wouldn't even notice, they'd tie strings to my hands and feet like a puppet, they'd sit me on a chair. It'd be very handy – then I could fly around outside all round the world. I wouldn't have to worry about my body any more – it's more trouble than it's worth. Anne nudges me, pressing knives and forks into my hand.

'Hello!' she shouts. 'Earth to Malvina! Jesus, you're so annoying! Pull yourself together, it's Easter today, we don't all have to know how lovesick you are.'

'I'm not lovesick!' I grunt at her, although I'm not too sure about that.

Just to be on the safe side, I don't think about Screwy very often. I've put him in the drawer for unfinished business that isn't going to get finished, and shut it tight. My granddad's in there too. I know that's not fair, it's just there aren't that many drawers in my heart so I've decided Screwy and Granddad will just have to get along somehow, but most of the time they rant and rave in there. Especially Granddad, he's always hammering on the door; it seems as if the door's right behind my forehead, because I can hear the hammering all the time. It's quiet during the day, but at night it's so loud now I can't sleep, his voice and his fists wake me up. Then I feel sorry for Screwy. I bet he can't get a wink of sleep with all that noise.

Anne and I don't say a word to each other as we finish laying the table together, then Mum brings in the lunch and everyone sits down, Paul and Dad too. Paul winks at me but I just give him an unfriendly stare back; I'm like a foreign body in the midst of my family, like a stone in their shoe.

'What's the matter with you?' asks Paul, winking again.

'Just ignore her,' says Anne, 'she's been awful for days. Ever since her boyfriend turned up here.'

Under the table, I kick Anne as hard as I can.

'See!' she squeals. 'She's crazy!'

Dad gives both of us a stern look. He can't stand arguments at the table, he wants his peace and quiet while he's eating, especially at Easter when we're all together and Mum's not moaning about her migraines for once.

'There's something we have to talk about,' he says, and Anne immediately falls silent and looks at Dad in expectation. She probably hopes I'm going to be sent to boarding school, or better still to a desert island. Even I'm pretty interested in finding out what it is. Dad doesn't normally discuss things with us, he decides most things on his own because he knows what's good for us anyway. It'd be an absolute waste of time asking us for our opinion, he says, and making decisions would just be an added burden on Mum. Paul's the exception, he's a grown man after all, and he's at uni as well. Lizzy can work herself up about that kind of thing for hours. 'And what if nobody wants to go to Wales with him?' she says. We almost always go to Wales in the school holidays. I just shrug; Dad doesn't care if we want to or not.

'I'd hate Wales,' says Lizzy with conviction. She and her mother go somewhere different every time, they take an old VW camper van and pretend to be gypsies. Last time they went to Portugal and they were gone for seven weeks because the van broke down and the Portuguese mechanics took so long to fix it. Lizzy came back to school a week late; she was brown as a berry and her hair still tasted of salt. She didn't wash it specially, just so I could taste the salt. I wish I could go on holiday with Lizzy and her mother, but my parents won't let me. They say it's not the done thing, driving round the world in a van, and anyway children have to go on holiday with their own parents. I can hardly wait until I'm not a child any more, I'm just worried the blue camper van won't last that long. There's a few years to go yet, but Lizzy says that doesn't matter, they'll just buy another old van if that happens, specially for me.

Dad puts his knife and fork down beside his plate and clears his throat. I'm sitting diagonally opposite him and I can tell by his face that it's not about holidays, it's about something more important, it's about something he doesn't want to talk about himself. I can tell, and an ice-cold fist of fear clenches in my stomach.

'You all know your granddad's not in the best of health,' he says. 'He hasn't been the same since Gran died.'

I take a quick look at Paul. He carries on eating regardless, bending over his plate, shovelling a piece of meat into his mouth and chewing.

'Your mother and I have agreed he can't cope on his own any more.'

I almost laugh out loud. Your mother and I! My mum doesn't give a shit about Granddad, she hates him, she never thinks about him, and when she does it's nothing good, she'd never worry about him. Never.

'We've decided he's going to move in with us. He can have Paul's room,' says Dad.

For a moment I think the fist is clenching my stomach together so tightly I'm going to vomit, right here at the dinner table.

'I don't believe you,' I say and try to catch Mum's eye.

'You didn't decide that,' I say to her. 'You hate Granddad, you'd never want him to live with us. No one wants that! No one!'

I stand up slowly and press my hands to my belly. Everything's hurting; it feels as if the piece of meat I swallowed five minutes ago was eating up my stomach, as if someone had given me acid to drink instead of apple juice.

'Don't be silly, Malvina,' says Paul.

He puts his fork down too at last.

'Where else could Granddad go? We're all he's got.'

'He can go to an old-people's home,' I say in a flat voice. 'That's what old-people's homes are for.'

I know how stupid that sounds, it sounds cold and unfeeling – exactly the way I feel. The others don't say anything at all. Dad shakes his head and Paul narrows his eyes to little slits. He hasn't been angry with me much before, almost never. Once when I broke a present his girlfriend gave him, a key ring; he was really angry then but only for a little while because I was so young. I was scared he'd never like me again, he'd never whirl me around in the air and talk to me, and now I'm scared again. So much is messed up already. I've been running down a passageway and slamming doors behind me. Lots of doors, so many that I'm afraid no one will ever be able to open them all again. Especially not Paul. Not Dad either. And Mum and Anne don't count. They weren't there. I don't know why, but there was only ever Gran, Granddad and me. Why not Anne? Why did Anne get out of it? I take another step back.

'You don't want this,' I say to Mum.

I don't even know myself what I mean exactly – that she doesn't want him to move in, or that she doesn't want him to kiss me, touch me, come in my room. Once he lives here I'll never be safe. He'll come in my room at night and in the bathroom when I'm in the shower, he'll lie in wait for me round every corner, every second, every day until he dies.

Mum just shrugs helplessly; when Dad decides something that's how it's done, we all know that. I haven't got much time left to avert disaster. To be precise, I have as long as lunch on Easter Sunday and not a second longer – once this is over there'll be no going back. Then Granddad will move in quicker than I can count to three. The very idea shoots holes in my head, it stops me from thinking clearly. I search feverishly for explanations, for words that express what's locked inside me, words I can say without dying of shame. As I'm struggling for these words Paul's eyes rest on me; he's leaning back in his chair, his arms folded across his chest. I'm not brave. I'd have to be very brave to say what I want to say and put up with his eyes on me like this at the same time.

'He kisses me,' I say and feel them shrinking back from me. They don't want to hear what I say, and if they did I'd have to be clearer, much clearer. It's not enough that he kisses me, it's not nearly enough. I'd have to say that he puts his hands on my breasts and sticks his tongue in my mouth, that he does things I refuse to even think about, let alone do. Maybe that still wouldn't be enough. Maybe they still wouldn't understand.

'Don't be so prissy,' says Anne. 'Little Miss Don't-Touch-Me!'

She starts laughing, and Paul and Dad join in. Relieved because it's all as simple as that and because they don't have to think about what I'm saying.

'It's just a phase,' says Dad, sounding very understanding, as if I was ill. Understanding and compassionate. Paul nods and starts eating again, grease shining on his chin, and I suddenly find everything repulsive.

'When is he moving in?' asks Paul.

'As soon as possible,' says Dad. 'He has to give notice on his flat, and then we'll save money on his rent, and that's good for all of us.'

They don't take any notice of me. They act like nothing has happened, only Mum pokes nervously at her food. She's gone white in the face again, but she doesn't say anything. She wouldn't even say anything if I grabbed her and shook her until her teeth chattered, until she fainted or started screaming. But my arms are like rubber, hanging lifeless at my sides, and I don't even have the strength to hold my knife and fork.

Granddad's moving in with us. The words chase around my head and make everything else pale, there are no colours any more, only spots of light in a darkness that's getting larger and larger. Granddad's moving in with us, his room will be at the other end of the hall, he'll be standing by my bed when I wake up in the morning and when I fall asleep at night, and there won't be a peaceful minute without him in between. I'll take him to school with me in my head and to Lizzy's, he'll wind himself around me tighter and tighter until there's nothing left of me. No one will notice anything because I'll carry on working, just like I'm still working now, and because they don't want to notice, and there's no solution for any of it. None. No way out.

They've been talking about something else for ages, I've blown my chance because I wasn't brave enough, because I didn't have the guts to slam the truth in their faces. They're talking about Paul's uni. He's doing business studies, he wants to work in a big bank. He's telling funny stories about his lecturers and the other students; they don't take any notice of me as I leave.

'It's her age,' I hear Paul saying. 'Leave her be, she'll calm down.'

I cycle all the way across to the estate. I don't know where Screwy lives but I'll find him. I comb through street after street looking for clues, but everything looks the same on the estate. Dead straight roads, terraced houses with square front gardens, all with the same blue and white striped awnings. On every block a play area: climbing frames, slides and swings. Everything is deserted. Of course, it's Easter, everyone's sitting at the table with their families for Sunday lunch before they go for a walk in the afternoon and on an Easter-egg hunt. And I'm hunting for Screwy.

I don't know what I want to say to him. As my eyes scan the rows of houses I work on my speech. *You've got to help me,* I'll say. That feels good. Just this sentence and Screwy's face as I say it lower my heartbeat.

You've got to help me, my best friend's not here and I don't know who else could help. But you can.

I decide against *but you can.* It sounds too dramatic. But it's true he's the only one. I don't know when Lizzy's coming back. The blue camper van hasn't got snow chains, and they've taken it up to the mountains. They might be stuck in a glacier and waiting for the thaw. As far as I know that can take ages. Maybe even as long as it takes Portuguese mechanics to fix a van, or even longer. I can't possibly wait for Lizzy.

'My granddad touches me,' I whisper, trying it out.

That chases my pulse right up, and I stop to stroke my hair out of my face. Pause. I'm going to have to practise this. I have to say that sentence lots and lots, so I can say it without stumbling.

'My granddad touches me. And I have to touch him.'

It's not going to work. I can't possibly say that. Not to Screwy. But it's the truth. 'It's the truth,' I whisper.

I search through my pockets for a hair slide and then pin back the strands of hair. The wind's too strong. I can't help thinking of Mrs Bitschek, how the wind billowed out her polka-dot skirt. How she said my granddad's a bad person.

'You have to hide me,' I whisper. 'You have to hide me in your cellar until my granddad's dead.'

That feels good too. He could bring me food every day and we'd lie on a mattress and hug. Every day. By the end I'd be really pale because I wouldn't have seen daylight for years. I'd have to wear dark glasses on the day my granddad died and I left the cellar again. I wouldn't take my sunglasses off all through the funeral, and instead of throwing flowers on the coffin I'd spit on it.

I can't find any sign of Screwy. No washing line with holey faded jeans hanging over it, and no scruffy trainers on any steps. I can't spot his bike either. If I don't find him on the next block I'll have to start again from the beginning, and ring every doorbell and ask for him. It could take years. One more block and one play area.

The playground is behind a box hedge. I can hear voices and a swing squeaking wildly. Then nothing more, and a dull thud.

'At least five metres,' someone shouts breathlessly.

'You idiot, that wasn't even three metres,' someone

else shouts back and breaks out in a barrage of laughter.

I spy through the hedge and spot Screwy, Puddle and Poker Face. It looks like they're practising jumping off the swing. Puddle's crouching in the sand, crossing his arms in a sulk.

'Five metres,' he repeats.

Now Screwy starts swinging. The swing squeaks like crazy – it sounds like it's going to break out of the ground any moment now, but Screwy goes on swinging until he almost goes over the top.

'Outta my way,' he shouts, and Puddle crawls out of the firing line, offended. He and Poker Face stand next to the square of sand at a suitable distance. Then Screwy jumps, he jumps off at the highest point, flaps his arms and really does get a bit further than Puddle.

What am I going to do now? The boys drop down onto the sand together. Screwy hands round a packet of cigarettes and they talk quietly; I can't make anything out. Cautiously, I let go of my bike and think about what to do. What have I got to lose?

'You've got to help me,' I whisper again, but now it feels stupid. With Puddle and Poker Face here – no way.

The entrance to the play area is on my left. All I have to do is walk in and ask Screwy if he's got a minute. I have to tell him I need to talk to him. It's as easy as that.

So I walk in. The boys don't spot me straightaway.

Then Poker Face sees me, gives the others a nudge with his foot, and Screwy and Puddle both turn round to me.

My heart's nearly standing still, I can't get a word out. Screwy stares at me in disbelief. He doesn't smile, he just stares, and I walk over to the swing. Past the boys, not saying anything. Not even hello, nothing.

Oh my God! Oh my God! Oh my God!

'What does she want here?' grunts Poker Face, and I see Screwy shrug.

'No idea,' he says.

Puddle grins, not letting me out of his sight. The other two carry on talking, whispering together, and I'm so embarrassed I start swinging. Higher and higher, even though my stomach's bound to start churning any minute now. I don't feel too good on swings, in fact not on anything like that, roundabouts or roller-coasters, I always feel sick straightaway. But I don't care about that right now. Screwy doesn't look in my direction once; he acts like he doesn't know me; maybe he's even ashamed to admit it.

You've got to help me, I think, congratulating myself on my own stupidity.

The world rushes past me; every time the swing swings back I feel like my stomach slips down to my knees. I can't see the boys any more, I can just hear them laughing. At the highest point, I jump. For a moment everything seems to stand still; I rotate my arms and the momentum carries me out over the sand, much further than Screwy and Puddle jumped, maybe because I'm so light. I crash-land on a trampled-down patch of grass, and a sharp pain flashes up my right arm. It must be broken, I think, but seeing as I don't need to cry I abandon the idea again. Lizzy says you can't help crying when you break something. Taking no further notice of the boys, I leave the play area with dignity. At least I hope so, but the minute I get behind the hedge I start running. Screwy catches me up on his bike.

'What was that all about?' he barks. 'You could have broken every bone in your body.'

'Like you care!' I bark back, swinging onto my saddle.

'You don't have to prove anything to me,' he says, holding onto my handlebars. 'I know perfectly well you're crazy, you don't have to kill yourself to prove it.'

My wrist is throbbing so I can't push him away. I wait until he lets go of my handlebars of his own accord.

'What d'you want here?' he asks.

'I wanted to go on the swing,' is my snotty answer, and I feel pretty stupid as I say it.

He jams my front wheel between his legs as well so I can't leave. Now would be the right moment, the moment to tell him he's got to help me. I let it go by. Puddle and Poker Face are rustling in the hedge behind me.

'OK,' says Screwy. 'I see.'

He lets go of the handlebars, freeing up my exit.

'By the way, they're tearing down the villa next week,' he says.

I nod. 'I heard that too,' I say.

I wish I was braver, but I'm not. I'm never going to be able to tell him about me, I won't ever be able to tell anyone about me. About me and Granddad.

I ride slowly back through the estate. The wind is playing with the awnings and the brightly coloured little windmills in the front gardens. My wrist is hurting like hell but I still don't have to cry. Everything's cold inside me. Somehow I stayed up in the air when I jumped off the swing. I haven't come back to my shell. I'm flying up to the stars. Too far away to reach me.

Monday

If you haven't got a pond, a water butt is the best thing that can happen to you. Lizzy and I climbed into the barrel and carefully felt across the bottom with our feet. The edge was slimy with algae. Sometimes we stroked against sharp edges and we had to watch out that our knickers didn't get caught on them, but all in all we thought the idea with the water butt was an absolute hit.

'Much better than the attic,' said Lizzy.

It was such a tight fit in the barrel I could feel her legs against mine, and that was kind of a good feeling, as if the two of us belonged together, really steady and inseparable.

'Lizzy,' I said, 'we'll always be friends, won't we?'

I was so scared that Lizzy might suddenly make herself scarce, find another friend to talk to and laugh with and get up to no good with.

'You don't half ask stupid questions,' she said, flashing a look at me from below – Lizzy's a tiny bit shorter than me. She was still wearing her eye patch back then, so she could only flash a look out of one eye, but that was enough.

'Of course we'll always be friends – blood sisters and friends,' she said.

Then she ducked underwater. She had to hold her nose and snort like a walrus, and when she came back up again she had duckweed all over her head and her eye patch had slipped out of place.

'Thank God,' she snorted. 'My brain nearly over-heated. You gotta go underwater too, it looks mad down there!'

An overheated brain was no laughing matter, so both of us went underwater at the same time and tried to keep our heads under for as long as possible. When we came up again, laughing and out of breath, we looked into four grinning faces.

That wiped the smiles off our lips.

Right by the barrel were Screwy, Puddle, Poker Face and Hubba Bubba.

'How cute,' said Screwy, 'two little mermaids.'

'How cute,' retorted Lizzy, 'four complete idiots.'

And then there was silence for a while, as we realised that we'd definitely got ourselves into a tricky situation. We were perched in a water butt with nothing on but knickers and trainers. Around the barrel were the boys, and behind them our shorts and matching men's vests were dangling from an apple tree. In short, we weren't exactly in a position to defend the villa or get into a skirmish with the boys – not even to get out of the barrel.

I wondered what time it must be and tried to work out how many hours we'd be trapped in the butt. The boys would have to go home too at some point, I thought, but if the worst came to the worst that could be hours from now, and by then we'd almost certainly have turned blue, grown webbed toes and caught our deaths of cold.

Screwy propped himself up with both elbows on the edge of the barrel, and we pressed our arms to our not yet existent breasts. I could have died of shame.

'So,' he said, 'where's your leader now, eh?'

Yeah, where was he? I thought. I couldn't think of anything, of course. I couldn't magic one up, could I? Lizzy had no stroke of inspiration either. Her lips formed a thin line and her eye was dark with rage.

'You'd better bugger off before he comes,' she said.

Screwy grinned.

'Shall I tell you what?' he said, bending further forward in a pally way, 'There is no leader. There's only you two. And you're trapped in a rain barrel.'

Then he turned back to the other boys.

'Search the villa!' he said.

The boys moved out while Screwy kept watch on our barrel. He had his stupid grin on his face the whole time. It took ages for them to get through all the rooms, and Lizzy and I had goose pimples on our arms and all over our bodies.

'There's no one here,' Poker Face finally yelled from a room on the first floor. 'It's all empty.'

Screwy grinned even more idiotically. He fished our clothes off the apple tree.

'Have fun getting home!' he said.

To the boys' malicious jeers, we climbed out of the water barrel with as much dignity as possible and marched off. Lizzy threw her head back but I knew she was feeling as miserable as I was. I could feel the boys' eyes on my bare back and my bum, and I thanked God that my knickers weren't white and see-through. Water squelched out of our trainers at every step; it was a terrible exit.

When we turned back to the villa again from the little hill, we saw the boys had taken in our pirate flags. Instead, our shorts and vests were hanging out of the windows.

'That's the limit!' said Lizzy. 'The absolute limit!'

From my bedroom doorway, I watch Paul clearing out his room. He packs his books in boxes, getting rid of loads of them – old fantasy books, *The Hobbit* clattering to the floor along with scruffy paperbacks, detective stories, magazines – he doesn't keep much. He ends up with just two boxes, full of books and odds and ends that come together in abandoned bedrooms when you move out. Everything else lands up in the bin. I'm sitting in my bedroom doorway with my legs folded underneath me, not letting him out of my sight. If he's going to run off and leave me alone with

Granddad, he'll have to put up with me. He'll have to put up with me punishing his every move with contempt. He manages to ignore me for at least an hour, then he loses his nerve and turns round to me.

'You're not going to change anything,' he says.

He comes down the hall over to me and kneels down. I don't answer. I'm floating below the ceiling like a helium balloon, watching him.

'You've really changed,' says Paul. 'I can hardly tell it's you. What's the matter? Is it true what Anne says, that you're in love?'

I don't respond, and he sighs and takes my hands in his. They feel warm and soft. I sense his warmth flowing over to me, and I long to roll myself up in his lap like a kitten. Paul doesn't notice any of that of course; my hands are clammy, there's nothing coming back from me.

'Why are you shutting yourself off like this?' he says. 'We used to have such good talks. I always helped you as well as I could.'

He sighs again, pressing my hands slightly.

'If it's about that boy,' he says, 'Anne told me about him.'

I try to stay calm even though I don't want to hear about it. Screwy's history. I messed it all up. He's disappointed in me because I'm so funny and I can't talk to him. It's all my fault. I should have told him the truth yesterday, or the day before, or last week. Or I should have pulled myself together, pretended everything's fine. Acted like the normal Malvina. It's too late now anyway. I could tell by his face yesterday, he doesn't want anything to do with me now.

'Anne told me he came round,' Paul says, and then he stops for a minute. He wants to give me a chance to answer, but I don't. My lips are sealed shut.

'She says he seems to like you.'

I'm glad I'm floating by the ceiling like a helium balloon, it means I don't have to really feel what's going on inside me. Everything's muffled, even Paul's voice, and the things he says only get through to me up here slowly. *Screwy seems to like me.* The idea washes around me like a swarm of bubbles. Carbon dioxide in a glass of water. It fizzes up the edges and gathers around me.

'She says he wanted to see you, and you just ran off out the back door. Because you thought he was flirting with her.'

'He *was* flirting with her,' I say quietly.

Anne's door opens next to me. She seems to have been eavesdropping; first a strand of her blonde hair swings through the gap, then the whole of her freckled face appears.

'He wasn't,' she says, and her voice has an insulted undertone to it. 'Anyway, I don't flirt with younger boys. That'd be so embarrassing.'

She wrinkles her nose in disgust.

'You didn't even want to know what he said.'

She pushes herself through the gap and plumps down on the floor next to us. I don't trust her. Up to now, there's always been a catch with Anne. If you borrow her T-shirt she wants an ice cream in return, if she helps you with your homework you can just wait till you have to throw yourself into the breach for her. It's all right in general to help each other out, but it has to be voluntary. Anne's favourite line is *I scratch your back, you scratch mine*. Lizzy says Anne's just a bad person, and that only gets worse with age. So now I'm waiting for the catch.

'D'you want to know or not?' she says.

I lower my chin to my chest. She doesn't have to say anything, I don't care.

'Of course she wants to know,' says Paul.

He presses my hands again. Like a buddy, like we got on really well and had a shared secret. The three of us, all together in the hall. But those days are long gone now. We're not a team any more. We're not playing Titanic in our old Ford and telling ghost stories in bed. All of us have changed, and maybe Paul's right and I've changed worst of all. I'm not their little Malvina any more, the girl you can tell fairy tales to and pass them off as the truth, fairy tales that end happily ever after with the princess finding justice. There's no such thing as fairy tales like that. At least not in my life.

I'm Malvina with the dark secret, Malvina with the many lives, I'm Malvina in the bathtub.

'He said you're the moodiest cow he's ever met, but he likes you anyway.'

The bubbles fizz around my head, tickling my throat and going up my nose.

'Sorry,' says Anne, 'but that's exactly what he said.'

Paul lets go of my hands. He's got to get on with his packing, hasn't he?

'You see,' he says before he goes back to his room, 'It was all a big fuss about nothing.'

Anne taps me cautiously on the foot.

'You can borrow my red T-shirt if you want to go and see him, the one with the mermaids on, I bet it'd suit you.'

I know that's a peace offering. I nod and wait for Anne to find the T-shirt; it's her favourite top and she drops it in my lap.

'Have fun,' she says.

'Good to see you here.'

I'm sitting under the guardian angels in their gold frame, and Mrs Bitschek is standing at the cooker making something out of meat and vegetables. There's an intense smell of fennel, slightly sweet, but also of black pepper and crushed garlic.

'Good to see you here,' she says again. 'I was waiting, I look in crystal ball every day – no Malvina – but then this morning, I think, thank God, at last! I thought you are not coming any more. Thought it is too late.'

I don't know what she means by that and she doesn't turn round to explain, just carries on stirring at the cooker. She's fastened her baby to her chest with a big, brightly patterned cloth. He sneezes now and then when he gets too much pepper in his nose, but otherwise he's unusually happy. He puts his chubby little hands in his mouth and drools on Mrs Bitschek's blouse.

'Where's Bratko?' I ask. I can't spot him anywhere.

'Oh him,' she says, 'he's got girlfriend, nothing in his head but walking over roofs and making kittens. Eating and kittens.'

I can't help grinning. I can't imagine Bratko like that. How would that big fat cat get up onto the roofs? I tuck my legs underneath me, feeling cosy. Dots of light play across my face, and Mrs Bitschek puts a bowl of steaming vegetables down on the table in front of me.

'Eat!' she says. 'Thin little birdy.'

She gives my hair a quick stroke and then sits down on the bench opposite me, untying the baby.

The stew is delicious, the best thing I've eaten for ages. Maybe it tastes so good because I haven't eaten much at all recently. I'm so hungry I could eat a horse. Mrs Bitschek watches me shovelling down the stew; it's so hot I burn my tongue, but I don't mind.

'You ask me about childhood,' she says, 'down in yard, remember? Last Thursday.'

She doesn't wait for me to answer, just keeps on talking and rocking the baby on her knees.

'I thought about it, and I thought of something, a story, I want to tell you it. That's why I wait for your visit. Story from my childhood, long ago.'

She looks out of the window as if she could read the story there, as if there were letters on the windowpane and she had to try hard to decipher them. Or she doesn't know how to start, how her story begins.

'I had a friend,' she says after a while, 'in Poland, best friend. We lived in a tiny village. Everyone knew each other, only ten or eleven houses, you understand? I lived in one house with Mama, Papa and six brothers, and next door lived Katja and Katja's papa and Katja's little sister. Katja's mama had gone away with a man from the next village, Katja was nine then. Her mama never came back.'

Mrs Bitschek looks for her story in the windowpane, and I spoon up my fennel. Bratko comes in the kitchen door. He looks incredibly ruffled and has a blood-lined scratch right across his nose. Perhaps from his girlfriend, I think, or from a rival.

'Until her mama went we play every day in yard together, go to school together and have secrets together. Like little girls do. But then...One day she doesn't come to school, just stays home, no one knows why. No one asks why. I do not ask why either. Maybe she's sick, I think. Next day too no Katja at school. After school I will go to her and ask, I think – but I don't ask. I meet her papa in yard, he sits there and reads newspaper. "Hello, how are you?" he says, and I stand there and don't dare to ask where is Katja.'

I put my spoon down beside my empty bowl. Mrs Bitschek's story is starting to make me feel uncomfortable. Her face looks sad and furrowed. The baby's fallen asleep.

'Next day Katja is there, at school. Sits next to me and doesn't talk. Looks pale, and I think, maybe still a bit sick. Maybe fresh air does her good, so I ask if we go play in fields. Together, like we did before every day. But Katja just says, "No, I can't," and when I ask why she says she must stay at home, she can't play any more every day because her mama is gone, and now she must do what her mama did before. That's how it was. No more playing. No more running in fields. Only work. From then, Katja doesn't come to school often. And when she's there we don't talk. Just sits next to me with white face and doesn't talk.'

Bratko jumps onto my lap. He's never done that before; he smells of sunshine and hot roofs, and he hunkers down on my knees. I'm glad about that; now I don't have to look at Mrs Bitschek any more. I wish she wouldn't finish the story. I don't want to know what happened to Katja. But Mrs Bitschek keeps talking, she can't seem to tell how uncomfortable I'm feeling – or maybe she can tell and that's why she keeps talking.

'Once she comes to school, wears long jumper in August, and I ask her, "You not hot?" And she says, "No, I'm OK." But later Katja washes her hands in toilets, I see she rolls up her sleeves... her arms are all covered in rash, and I'm too scared to ask why, and when Katja sees me she hides arms behind back, ashamed, she runs away. We're not friends any more. I have different friend, and Katja has nobody now.'

The silence hangs heavy between us as Mrs Bitschek stops talking. I stroke Bratko's dusty, warm fur mechanically. It's so quiet you can even hear the baby breathing, the baby and Bratko's purring. Then Mrs Bitschek starts again.

'Two years later Katja doesn't come to school at all. I see her often at the window. Once I wave, but she closes the curtains, very quickly. Her little sister plays outside sometimes, she is just turned eight, looks like Katja before, healthy and happy, sometimes I talk to her, but her papa doesn't like that, when he catches us he gets angry. Calls her into house. He does not beat her, she says, but she's still scared. Two more years later, both girls are dead. Someone finds them in forest, in the canyon. There are lots of canyons where I come from. They jumped into one. No one wants to know why. I know. All along I know. But I didn't say anything. Just as cowardly as all the others.'

She lays the baby down next to her on the bench, carefully. It doesn't wake up but pulls a face in its sleep.

'Why are you telling me this?' I say, hardly recognising my own voice, it sounds so unreal in my ears.

'My girl, my girl…' says Mrs Bitschek.

She reaches across the table for my arm but I pull it back with a jerk, such a jerk that it gives Bratko a shock and he hisses at me.

'You know too why they jumped. Katja was strong, took everything, all the nights with her father.

153

But she couldn't protect her sister. She thought dying is better...'

'Better than what?' I say.

'Better than life she had, and better than talking. You understand? You can only change things if you talk.'

'I don't understand,' I say, angry. 'I don't understand anything at all, I don't understand why you're telling me this terrible story, it's got nothing to do with me. You don't get it. It's got nothing to do with me, anything like that.'

I throw Bratko off my lap and jump off my chair, the baby wakes up and screams, the sound of my voice has woken him, he screams as if someone wanted to harm him, and Mrs Bitschek hurries to pick him up.

'Malvina,' she says, 'sit down, please...'

As I rush to the door she comes running after me, jamming her foot against the door as she doesn't have a hand free because of the baby.

'You must talk, Malvina,' she says urgently, then she lets go of the door, letting me out – into the arms of my granddad. He's standing in the corridor; maybe he's been listening at the door.

He drags me into his flat, pulling me by the wrist, the wrist I sprained yesterday. He's never hit me but now I'm suddenly scared he will, because I was round at Mrs Bitschek's, because of the story. He can't know about the story but he can tell. He can tell what Mrs Bitschek was talking to me about. He looks like a cornered animal. Volatile and angry.

'Never go round to that woman again!' he shouts.

He emphasises every single word overly clearly, yelling right in my ear.

'Do you understand me?'

We're standing in the living room, facing each other. He slammed the door behind us so no one can hear his shouts. He's breathing heavily; maybe he'll have a heart attack, I think, then it would all be over. All of it. All at once.

'Do you understand me?' he yells again, digging his fingers into my shoulders.

'Your gran wouldn't have wanted it,' he says, quieter this time, and his eye flickers dangerously.

'It was your fault what happened to Gran, you know that don't you? You do realise that?'

I can taste his stale breath in my face.

'It wasn't my fault,' I say, and I feel tears welling up inside me. I press them back down again, swallowing so they stay down in my stomach where they belong.

'Yes, it was, Malvina. Yes, it was.'

He starts pushing me slowly backwards towards the sofa.

'Everything was fine as long as we were happy, the three of us. You were happy, your gran was happy, and I was too. But then, then you brought that friend along, once, twice, then more and more. Do you remember, Malvina?'

I nod; I do remember that. Lizzy. The best friend in the world. She saved me. She showed up in my life and suddenly everything was all right. I could forget, and I certainly did forget, all right. Everything. All those Friday afternoons. Everything that had happened behind that locked bathroom door. And I could live again. I wasn't scared any more. But everything has its price.

'She died because of you,' says Granddad, 'because of you. You didn't want to make sacrifices any more. But you have to make sacrifices in life. You have to be there for other people. For people you love. You're going to have to learn that.'

'She had cancer,' I say helplessly.

Granddad looks at me full of contempt, then his expression changes, his face goes soft, he lets go of my shoulders and takes my face in his two hands.

'Yes, she did,' he say quietly, 'and you could have helped her, my little Malvina.'

With a tired movement, he strokes my cheeks, then he turns away. I hear his footsteps as he goes into the bathroom. The boiler lights up.

'I'll run a bath for us, Malvina,' he says, 'just like the old days.'

Tuesday

Lizzy. One day she was just there. She had a piano lesson with Mrs Neumann just before me. While I waited for my turn in the hall outside Mrs Neumann's music room, I could hear how badly Lizzy played. She never hit the right note, she hammered at the keys with great enthusiasm and drove Mrs Neumann from one desperation to the next. Her class was over at four on the dot, then she slipped out of the door like greased lightning and was gone, giving me a friendly grin but never staying to talk. The whole thing continued for a few weeks, lesson after lesson, and then she talked to me.

'I've nearly got her where I want her now,' she whispered before she ran down the stairs.

'Where?' I whispered back.

'She's nearly ready to chuck me out,' said Lizzy.

From then on she kept me up to date on the state of play. She told me her mother had started work as a teacher at a music-focused nursery school, and since then she was obsessed with her daughter Lizzy profiting from it.

'I said I wanted to learn the drums,' said Lizzy, 'but she wasn't having any of it.'

Every time we met in the hallway we had a quick chat, but only as long as it took Mrs Neumann to sort out her music and clean the piano keys with disinfectant. Mrs Neumann's got a bit of a tic, you see. She feels constantly under threat from bacteria, so she disinfects her piano after every lesson.

Up to the day when Mrs Neumann really did throw Lizzy out we never thought of meeting up anywhere else, but that day Lizzy waited for me. Even though it was winter and she froze her bum off in the ice-cold stairwell.

'Hi,' she said. 'What d'you say, I made it!'

We grinned at each other, and then I took Lizzy with me to Gran and Granddad's, as if she'd always walked the couple of yards to my grandparents' block with me. We swayed our music bags and bombarded each other with snowballs – everything was great with Lizzy.

At Gran's we helped each other with our homework – she was better at maths and I was better at English. We found out we lived not far apart, but Lizzy went to a different school to me – a private school that her dad paid for because he had a guilty conscience about the thing with Annabelle. She said it's fine for him to pay for her school – she prefers that to him hanging around at home with them. Later we heard Granddad coming home, and Gran disappeared into the kitchen. She looked nervous and said she had to do the washing-up, but the washing-up was all done already, she just didn't want to get in Granddad's way.

'Where's my little Malvina?' he called, and Lizzy started giggling. She tapped her forehead.

'He's a bit odd, isn't he?' she whispered.

I moved closer to her because now I was scared after all, but there was no need. Granddad came in and saw the two of us sitting at the table and he didn't dare to make a scene in front of Lizzy. He was really friendly, brought us chocolate and sweets, and then he sat down in his armchair and watched us.

I had won.

From then on Lizzy came with me every week. We met downstairs at Mrs Neumann's, we went to Gran and Granddad's, and nothing happened, everything calmed down. I felt safe.

It won't be long before people are pushing their shopping trolleys along aisles full of colourfully packaged food right where I'm standing now. They won't know that the ground was once strewn with daisies and dandelions, they won't know that little animals once built their nests in the many nooks and crannies of the villa and the pigeons lived up in the beams. They won't have any idea of all that, they'll stand at the checkout and get annoyed because the queue's moving much too slowly, because they're spending too much money as usual and their kids are whining. There's nobody here now. The wind has died down, soon April will be over and summer will shimmer above the meadows and burn the skin on my shoulders.

I climb the steps to the attic and try to memorise everything so I don't forget a single thing: the creaking of the wood, the cracks in the walls, the smell of fire that still lingers in the rooms on the first floor. Evil Frederick. I take the picture out of its frame, fold it in half twice and put it in my pocket. I don't want to forget anything, I want everything to stay preserved inside of me, unchanged. All the stories, the sound of us running down the stairs barefoot. Lizzy's laughter between the beams and the cooing of the pigeons.

I fall backwards with my eyes closed, onto my mattress with its pile of cushions. I can't believe it'll all be gone. Even the smell will disappear, instead it'll smell of cleaning fluid and exhaust fumes and air conditioning.

Screwy, I think, Screwy, Screwy, Screwy.

I wish he was here to drive away my dark thoughts. The villa, my granddad, Mrs Bitschek, her story yesterday.

I can imagine how Katja felt when she jumped into the canyon with her little sister. No way out.

No rescue. Alone. I can see the two of them before me, running along a little path, Katja ahead, determined, pulling her sister behind her, uphill, higher and higher, the little girl can hardly keep up, but Katja won't stop for a rest. She's turned off her thoughts, at some point she found the switch. Off. He'd gone too far, he'd come out of her sister's room one morning, yawning, with sleep still in his eyes. He bumped into her in the hall, pushed her out of the way. She heard her sister crying, quietly, just a whimper like a little injured animal. She launched into him with her fists. You swine, she yelled, you swine! And now she's rushing up the hill, and her little sister weighs a hundred kilos on her arm. Perhaps the sun is setting as they reach the top; you can't see the stones from where Katja and her sister are standing but Katja knows where they are. A straight part, fifty metres long, with moss and lichen growing on the stones, and then they fall away abruptly, a hundred-metre drop. 'We have to run,' says Katja, 'close your eyes and run.' Her sister's not scared, it's a game for her, she trusts Katja, so she runs as fast as she can, laughing and spreading out her arms.

Then they fly.

Their dresses billow out, it's perfectly silent among the rocks.

A shadow falls across my face, just like two weeks ago.

'What d'you want here?' I say, not opening my eyes.

'How's your arm?' asks Screwy.

I hold up my arm. The joint is swollen; I should have put cream on it, then it wouldn't be so bad now. Screwy touches the swelling; his fingers are cool and dry.

'At least you didn't break anything,' he says. 'I thought we'd have to call an ambulance when you jumped so far. I've never seen anyone jump such a long way.'

'Me neither,' I say, and I can't help grinning.

I open my eyes. Screwy is still holding onto my hand; he's sitting on the mattress next to me and I don't want to pull my hand away. It's all right for him to hold onto it. It doesn't hurt so much then. Well, maybe I'm just imagining that.

'Have you been practising?' he asks.

'Nah,' I say, 'I'm a natural at swing long jump. Once I've polished up my landings I'm joining the circus.'

He strokes the back of my hand with his thumb; he doesn't dare do anything more, and I wouldn't advise him to either. I'm like a wildcat. Always on my guard, all my senses sharpened and ready to leap. He knows that, that's why he's careful. Slowly, not letting go of my hand, he lies down next to me on his back, my hand on his chest; I can feel his heartbeat. We lie there and watch the clouds moving above us, appearing weightlessly above the roof and crossing our line of vision.

'D'you want to know my name now?' I ask, surprising myself.

Screwy's surprised too. He turns his face to mine; there's a tiny feather caught in his eyelashes.

'Malvina,' I say, 'the custodian of rights.'

That's the true meaning of my name. I'm the keeper of justice, and, as I say the words looking into Screwy's face, I realise for the first time what it really means. What it really means to be a custodian of rights. It means I have to take care of my rights, my right to live, the right to defend myself, the right to talk. I have to protect myself. It all sounds so simple with Screwy lying here beside me, as if all I had to do is go out and start straightaway. Screwy makes me feel strong, but what happens when Screwy's not here?

'Malvina,' he says, 'Malvina, the champion swing long jumper.'

We both have to laugh, and Screwy turns on his side so he can see me better. The mattress gives way beneath him and I roll a tiny bit closer to him. It's a bit embarrassing, at least it is to me – it seems to be perfectly normal to Screwy for us to be lying side by side and holding hands. He doesn't look nervous at all.

'In the beginning I thought you were just putting it on,' he says, 'but now I'm starting to think you're just like that.'

'Like what?' I say.

'You know, the way you are, crazy and jumpy, sometimes you're nice and sometimes you make me want to puke.'

'Thanks,' I say, rather offended.

So that's what he thinks I'm like, I make him want to puke.

'I didn't mean it like that,' he says quickly. 'You're usually nice … It's just, a lot of the time I don't understand why you're like that.'

He props himself up on one elbow. His hair, not in a ponytail today for a change, strokes across my face. I'm glad it's starting to get dark up here, it means he can't see that I'm blushing bright red with embarrassment. It's not every day a boy tells me I'm nice.

'You're nice too,' I say, going even redder.

'If they weren't going to tear down the villa we could have shared it,' says Screwy. 'You, your friend, my friends and me.'

'Lizzy hates you,' I answer. 'She'd never do that in a million years.'

It's true. I'm afraid Lizzy's going to have a fit when I tell her about Screwy. She'd never have shared the villa. I don't think so anyway. I'm really scared of the moment when I have to tell her what happened in the Easter holidays. And I'm going to have to tell her.

'We did some pretty dumb stuff last year,' says Screwy.

'Yeah, especially you lot,' I say. 'That thing with the rain butt was really mean.'

The sky above us is gradually turning pink; it'll soon be dark. My parents are probably worrying about where I am, but I don't care. Maybe they'll ring Granddad and he'll tell them I left at half-past six, right on time. I hope he's worried too, I hope he's really scared something might have happened to me. I hope he's so scared he can't sleep all night.

'Do you have to go home?' says Screwy, as if he'd just read my thoughts.

I shake my head.

'Do you?'

'I'll stay as long as you stay,' he says, pulling the curtain over the two of us like a bed cover.

It's cosy and warm between the fieldmice cushions. I roll onto my side and nestle my back against Screwy's chest, feeling his breath on my neck and his arm on my hip. He doesn't try to kiss me, we just lie there next to each other. Soon enough, the dusk swallows up all the contours; only the pigeons stand out as dark dots against the sky.

'Are you going to tell your friend about us?' asks Screwy.

'What should I tell her?' I ask back. For one fearful second I'm scared Screwy's angry or thinks there's nothing to tell.

'You know,' he says.

I can tell he's smiling, and the tip of his nose touches the back of my neck, very softly. It gives me goose pimples all over. Tips of noses on backs of necks are the best thing in the world, I decide. I'll have to tell Lizzy that, for one thing.

'Of course I'll tell her *you know*,' I say.

Then it's quiet again, it seems that's sorted everything out between us. We don't need to say anything more; Screwy holds me in his arms and the pigeons doze above us.

We're going to hold a vigil; that's what you do when someone dies, and we're holding a vigil all night because the men are coming to tear down the villa in the morning. Screwy says it's like paying our last respects to the villa, and it certainly deserves them. We pass the time by telling each other stories from our lives. Screwy tells me about his parents; they're getting divorced even though they've only just bought their house on the estate. 'They thought they could save their marriage with the house,' he says. 'What a stupid idea.' But Screwy's not sad about it. He doesn't like the house anyway and he thinks his parents are pretty dumb too. Maybe he'll move away, he says, with his mother, because his father's even worse, he's always yelling and shouting. What he says about his father reminds me of my father. Maybe all fathers are the same. Maybe they start turning strange as soon as their wives have children, I think. Or they were always like that but nobody noticed before. I try to imagine Screwy with a balding head, but I just can't. Screwy's different, he's never going to turn out like other grown-ups. Just like Lizzy and me. We're not going to be like that either. We're going to watch out for each other, Lizzy for me and me for Lizzy, and I can always watch out for Screwy as well if I have to.

'I'll be eighteen in two years,' he says. 'Then I'm moving out anyway.'

He tells me about Poker Face, Puddle and Hubba Bubba, whose names are completely different in real life, of course. Poker Face is his best friend, his very best friend. Screwy doesn't care what the others say but he thinks Poker Face likes me. My jump off the swing yesterday really impressed him, he reckons.

'Maybe we can fix him up with your friend,' says Screwy, but I don't think that's a very good idea. Lizzy would kill me if I tried to match-make for her. She'd break off our friendship.

I don't talk as much as Screwy. I take a careful detour around anything to do with Granddad, and I don't talk about my gran either. But I do tell him all about Lizzy. I tell him so much that Screwy gets scared and interrupts me.

'But we'll still see each other even if Lizzy doesn't like me...' he says.

I don't know where I find the courage. It comes from deep down or from far up, depending on what direction you're looking from. It probably comes straight from God, if there is a God. Anyway I turn around to face Screwy. I hug him really tight, as tight as I can, so that he knows I really mean it.

'I promise,' I say.

Screwy presses his face into the small of my neck. He doesn't know I don't usually make promises. Not even to Lizzy. Not to anyone.

We do fall asleep at some point, even though we wanted to stay awake and even though there's so much to talk about and I can't get enough of Screwy's voice. The curtain is wrapped around us like an airy, woven cocoon. We're little caterpillars, nestled together and waiting to transform, and the villa is a huge sleeping animal. It conceals us in its last night, and the moon hangs high above the trees.

wednesday

I can remember the exact moment when my anger at Screwy blew over. My fist hit his nose, making a tiny cracking sound that only the two of us heard. Or maybe we didn't hear anything at all and my imagination's playing tricks on me – it was actually much too noisy for tiny cracking sounds.

Lizzy was yelling, the boys were scrambling through the kicked-in door, and Screwy's blood spread across the floor and onto my T-shirt. My anger blew over.

Through the veil that time spreads over events when everything happens too quickly and you stand at the edge as if you had nothing to do with it all, I saw Screwy raise his arm and press his hand to his face. He staggered backwards as if in slow motion, falling against Puddle's chest and Puddle against Poker Face, then they turned round and stumbled out through the hole in the door.

169

Lizzy and I looked at each other.

'What if they come back?' I whispered.

We pushed and shoved an old chest of drawers in front of the hole. Not a sound came through from outside.

'Oh God, I think you broke his nose,' said Lizzy.

I thought so too. Lizzy said he'd probably need an operation. She said the boys wouldn't come back because they'd be taking Screwy to hospital. We imagined them pushing him along neon-lit corridors into an operating theatre, where they'd patch his nose back together again.

'My parents'll kill me if they find out,' I said.

'My mother'll kill me too,' said Lizzy, 'you know what she thinks about violence.'

We consoled each other with the thought that at least neither of us would survive the next few days if Screwy told on us. It wasn't much consolation. We were still young after all; we had so many exciting things ahead of us.

'I haven't even started my periods yet,' said Lizzy. 'It's so tragic.'

'Me neither,' I said.

We'd never talked about our periods before, and I was suddenly incredibly relieved that Lizzy hadn't started hers either. I think Lizzy felt the same way.

It was really a sin to die before you had your period and proper breasts, we decided. Only nipples, and that didn't count.

'And we've never fallen in love,' said Lizzy.

That was the worst thing by a long shot. You couldn't just die before you'd ever fallen in love. That was absolutely impossible.

'Dear God,' I said, 'please don't let Screwy tell on us.'

Lizzy nodded.

'And please make sure they get his nose back in working order,' she added.

I don't know if it had anything to do with our prayer, but Screwy didn't tell on us. We waited for days for something bad to happen. For the police to come and pick us up from home for grievous bodily harm. That was nonsense of course, but we were still scared. We ran to the villa every afternoon and watched the bloodstains gradually fading and mingling with the colour of the wood. At some point we forgot about the boys, and the summer holidays were over.

The diggers come at dawn. They roll slowly down the hill like angular yellow monsters. The noise wakes us up, the screaming of the engines and the crunching of the fence as they simply drive over it, as if it wasn't fence posts but toothpicks. Screwy and I pull off the curtain.

'Quick,' says Screwy. 'Get up!'

I don't know what he's planning, I just stand stunned at the window and watch the machines burrowing through the garden. They transform the supple grass into brown, flattened holes in the earth, and their shovels tear the bark off the trunks of the apple trees. Screwy is dragging things around the room behind me. I turn around and see that he's laid loose planks across the opening to the stairs.

'Help me with this,' he says.

The two of us drag the mattress to the hatch and pull it over the planks. The mattress is heavy, I remember dragging it up here on my own. That must be ages ago, I think, maybe a hundred years ago. The last stretch was the worst because the staircase is so narrow. I had to press myself up against the mattress with all the strength I had. It's easy peasy with Screwy now.

Outside, the engines die down. We hear men's voices but we can't understand what they're saying; they're laughing together. I sit down cross-legged on the mattress and I'm a bit scared they'll just blow up the villa with us inside it.

Boom! Everything will go flying all around us and we'll be buried under the masonry. The people in the supermarket might talk about it on the sly as they queue at the deli counter: 'Remember that young couple who died here, wasn't that terrible, a terrible shame...' It'd give them the creeps but they'd find the whole thing romantic, almost as romantic as Romeo and Juliet.

'Wait here,' says Screwy, and then he climbs up into the beams, smooth and supple, up to the very top of the roof. The first rays of sunlight run across his figure as he balances on the highest point, the pigeons fluttering around him. It looks beautiful. He looks like a prince, the prince of the pigeons.

He stands perfectly still with his arms wide apart to keep his balance. The men haven't seen him yet, even though all they'd have to do is raise their eyes.

'Hey!' he yells once he's got his balance, and they all turn round towards his voice, searching the sky for him.

'Hey,' he shouts again. 'You can't tear the villa down! We're in here and we're not leaving!'

The men spot him, taking a few steps back and shading their eyes with their hands.

'Hey, kid, don't do anything stupid!' one of them shouts.

'You'll break your neck!'

Screwy shakes his head.

'We're not leaving,' he shouts back.

It's good not to give up the villa without a fight, and the fact that we're fighting fills me with excited pride. We're protecting the villa, Screwy and I, Screwy the prince of the pigeons and me, Malvina, the custodian of justice. It's just a shame Lizzy's not here. She wouldn't believe I'm being so brave.

'We'll give you five minutes! You'd better come out or there'll be trouble!' another man shouts.

Screwy just jumps down and lands right in front of me. We smile at each other; it's as if we were the only people in the world.

'We're squatters,' I whisper, taking his hand.

Screwy nods.

'It's a good idea, isn't it?' he asks.

'We might end up in prison if they catch us, but it was still a good idea,' I say.

Screwy's not worried.

'They won't catch us,' he says. 'We just have to be careful, like in the movies.'

It's quiet outside; the five minutes don't seem to be up yet. Now the rising sun dyes the whole attic red, as if angels had tipped cans of paint over us, pouring their sunlight into every corner, and I'm suddenly terribly grateful to be here with Screwy, and I think it's worth fighting. Just for the villa, the silence of the morning, the rising sun and Screwy's face, wrinkled from the fieldmice cushions.

'We're the good guys,' he says, 'and the good guys always win.'

We move closer and wrap our arms around each other. I put my legs over Screwy's legs and rest my head on his shoulder.

'D'you think we're heavy enough?' I whisper.

'Course,' says Screwy, 'I weigh nearly eleven stone.'

That reassures me, because I only weigh eight stone, and Paul's always calling me *flyweight,* and saying he could lift me up with his little finger. The builders out there are probably really strong. They have to lug sacks of cement around all day, don't they, and if I've got my sums right I'm not even as heavy as a single cement sack, so they'd easily push me out of the hatch, mattress and all. Luckily, only one of them can push at a time. The stairs to the attic are so narrow there's no room for two men at the same time. Especially not two builders, they're usually pretty fat.

'Can I ask you something, Malvina?' says Screwy.

He strokes my back in a smooth rhythm, in time with my breathing.

I nod, even though he can't see that of course, but he can tell. He goes on stroking my back and I think maybe he's forgotten what he wanted to ask, because he strokes me for quite a long time and doesn't say anything.

'Why do you really have to go to your granddad's?' he asks then, and the shock flashes ice-cold through my body. Screwy doesn't notice, he can't feel my breath curdle, my heart pounding beneath his hands.

Keep calm, I think, keep calm, he still doesn't know anything, and he's never going to find out.

And then I think: he that loves danger shall perish in it.

My mother says that a lot, to make me watch out for myself. I usually think it's a pretty stupid thing to say. I always answer, 'Mum, I can look out for myself!' But she doesn't believe me. She thinks I run from one disaster to the next.

Now the quote seems to fit perfectly. *He that loves danger shall perish in it*. If I'm with Screwy he's going to keep on asking. Over and over again. He won't let it go. That's just the way he is. How long will I be able to put him off? If I manage it for the next ten minutes I'll be doing pretty well.

'Are you asleep?' he says, seeing as I don't answer.

'Don't be silly,' I say. 'Maybe they're in the house now, I think I just heard something.'

That's not true of course, I just made it up so I don't have to answer Screwy's question. We prick up our ears. There's obviously no one inside the villa.

'I can't hear anything,' says Screwy.

His hands have stopped stroking me. They're resting somewhere below my ribs.

'Come on, tell me,' he says.

'It doesn't matter now,' I whisper in his ear. 'We shouldn't be making any noise anyway.'

'I've been thinking about it,' he whispers back. 'About how strange you were behind the laburnum bush, how you went all funny, and I've been thinking about what you said. It's all to do with your granddad.'

'You think too much,' I say. 'It can't be healthy.'

I don't quite manage the flippant tone of voice I was aiming at; something in my voice makes Screwy sit up and listen.

'I'm right, aren't I?' he says.

The stupid thing about the whole situation is that I can't get out of it. I can't run away, the builders are down there, and Screwy's holding onto me tightly; I don't think he's going to let me go.

'You're imagining things,' I say. 'I'm no funnier than other girls, it's got nothing to do with my granddad. He's just the same as other granddads, just a normal guy, sometimes he's annoying and sometimes he's quite nice…'

'We're coming in now!' someone shouts from outside.

The front door downstairs scrapes across the wooden floor. They look around every room, banging the doors open and stamping up the stairs.

'They're in the attic, boss,' one of them yells. 'They've barricaded themselves in up there.'

Now they're on the staircase. I wish I knew if our bums are poking out underneath the mattress. Screwy says they're not, well maybe his is but mine definitely isn't – it's much too small. We giggle a bit; we're rather nervous, and giggling's the best thing you can do.

'How many of them are there?' shouts the boss.

I picture him as short and stocky, with a pock-marked face and a black suit. He's the only one wearing a suit because he's the boss and he's allowed to order the others around while he sits in his limousine and has his shoes polished by a skinny little boy. I picture him as really mean and nasty; his voice echoes through the villa, unpleasantly piercing.

'If he gets hold of us he'll string us up by our feet like in a Western,' I whisper. 'I bet he's really mean.'

Screwy nods.

'Maybe he'll have us cemented alive into the supermarket foundations,' he says; that's the worst thing Screwy can imagine.

We feel someone pushing a shoulder against the mattress from below.

'Bet there's ten of 'em sitting on top,' he says. 'I hate bloody kids.'

'Listen, you up there!' shouts the boss. 'You come out of there right now, we haven't got all day. Go and play somewhere else and let the grown-ups get on with their work.'

I let go of Screwy's shoulder and tip my head back. The pigeons are strutting around on the beams, stretching their wings – it's time to get up, they coo at each other, it's time to fly away.

'I've had enough of this,' yells the boss. 'I'm dialling the police on my mobile. D'you hear me? If you don't come down now the police'll be here in ten minutes, and then your parents'll have to pick you up down the station. But if that's the way you want it, all right, it's not my problem.'

At first we don't think he's being serious, but he is. He talks quietly on the telephone, we can only make out a couple of words. Kids, he says, teenagers, and that we've barricaded ourselves in up in the attic. I'm not scared of the police. I know they won't catch us, we're the good guys, aren't we, and anyway we know the villa like the back of our hands. I slowly shift my weight off the mattress, slowly so that they don't notice down below that Screwy's alone on it with his nearly eleven stone. The beams creak beneath my feet as I creep across the attic over to the holes in the roof from where you can see out over the road, the track from the villa to the estate. Mist hangs above the fields, rooks are diving from the hedges into

178

the swathes of mist. I watch them until I spot the police car coming over the hill.

'They're coming,' I whisper.

Then we climb up into the beams, the way Lizzy and I did a thousand times to play tricks on the boys, or just for fun because taking the stairs is boring, stairs are for wimps. We climb along the beams onto the roof, balance along the rooftop, putting one foot in front of the other, quietly so they don't see us. We've taken our shoes off because it's easier to get a grip on the tiles with bare feet.

I can feel Screwy behind me, it makes me dizzy and I have to really watch out I don't put a foot wrong. I can feel his smile on the back of my neck. Like goose pimples.

An old walnut tree leans against the villa here; we dangle in its branches like squirrels. They're strong, they can even take Screwy's weight, and it's easy to get down from the tree. We hear the men trampling around the villa. Maybe they're just pushing the mattress aside, now that we're sliding down the trunk and running to the fence, ducked down. We run until we can't see the villa any more, the damp morning sticking to our bare feet. I think of my curtain, the fieldmice cushions and the night we spent nestled together in the villa. It makes me sad and happy at the same time.

We have to split up just outside the estate. Screwy holds onto my hands.

'Don't let them get you down,' he says.

I shake my head.

'The good guys always win,' I say.

Screwy grins. He leans forward, we're both the same height, and his mouth meets mine rather clumsily but it still feels good. Soft and warm, like a fleeting ray of sunshine on my face. This time I don't push him away. I wait to see what happens, I wait until his lips pull away from mine, and I'm very proud of coping with being kissed without running away, and I think Screwy knows that I only stay put for his sake.

He can tell, because he really likes me.

I walk home slowly, my shoes dangling around my neck by their laces. I like the feeling of bare feet on the pavement, even though it's still cold and the road is damp with dew. I'm not in any rush to get home. I've never been out all night without letting my parents know, so I'm feeling pretty guilty. I bet Mum's gone half-mad with worry. She probably thinks I've been kidnapped, and I feel bad about that now, not like last night when I didn't care about anything and I thought I had to get back at them, make them just as sad as I am. Now I know them being sad wouldn't help me either. Maybe there's nothing that can help me, nothing anyone else does, maybe I have to do it myself and the people around me can watch. Lizzy, for one, and Screwy. They could stand behind me and I'd always know I'm not alone, and when I want to turn round and run away there'll be someone there to hold onto me.

I take the back way again, climbing over our garden fence onto the patio. I haven't got a key with me of course, and all the windows are shut apart from Anne's. I pull myself up by her window ledge.

'Anne,' I whisper through the gap. 'Anne, it's me!'

The pile of covers on top of my sister starts to move. She looks awful, her hair is sticking out in all directions, but I like her much better that way. She looks almost like she used to in the old days; in the old days, when we were still a team, wrestling in her bed and she always let me win even though she was much stronger than me. She pads across to the window, half-asleep, and that's a good thing too because I'm gradually running out of strength from hanging onto the window ledge.

'Where have you been?' she whispers as I drop down into her room, 'Were you out with that boy?'

I nod. Anne grins.

'I thought so,' she says.

'What's up with Mum?' I ask.

'She took a sleeping tablet at ten thirty because she couldn't stand worrying about you, and you're off to boarding school after the holidays. Congratulations,' says Anne, but this time it sounds friendly, not as if she really meant the bit about boarding school.

She hops back into bed.

'You can come in with me. They're bound to catch you if you walk along the hall,' she says, and I slip in under her covers even though my feet are dirty, and Anne doesn't say a single word of complaint.

'Tell me about the boy,' she says, and I tell her a little bit, not much because most of it's my secret, I don't want to tell Anne. Then we think about what to tell our parents, and Anne comes up with the idea that I could say I slept in her room. From eleven o'clock. That's incredibly nice of her, and I'm so grateful I decide I'll never call her *barn owl* again. Not unless she's really nasty.

Then Anne falls back to sleep, and I lie on my back. Maybe Anne would be another person who could stand behind me, I think, but I'm not quite that far yet, so I quickly think of Screwy instead. I can see his face above me on the ceiling.

'Don't let them get you down, Malvina,' he says. 'Just don't let them get you down.'

Thursday

She wanted to talk to me one last time before she died. On our own. She sent all the others away, out into the corridor: Mum, Dad, Anne and Paul. Granddad too of course. He spent most of the time in the corridor or in the toilet or in the cafeteria anyway. He couldn't look at Gran, he couldn't stand the way she was disappearing before our eyes, getting paler and paler as if they were wiping the colour out of her day by day. She was very weak, there were tubes in her arms. She wanted to die as soon as she stopped breathing, so she didn't have a mask over her nose or a tube in her mouth. My gran was always a very sensible, practical person. She wasn't scared of dying; she'd told me what would happen when she wasn't in her body any more. There was no need to be scared, she'd told me, the pain would go away and she wouldn't be alone any more – the pain was the worst thing and the long nights lying awake in her bed with time to think.

'Malvina,' she'd said, two weeks before she went back into hospital, 'someone who can't breathe on their own any more shouldn't be kept alive. Do you understand?' I understood, but I hoped desperately that she'd keep breathing on her own, that she'd recover just one more time like the other times she'd had to go into hospital, when they amputated her left breast and then her right one, pumped her full of drugs and then sent her home, scarred and a tiny bit smaller.

'I'm not going home again this time,' she said, once I'd sat down cross-legged at the end of her hospital bed. She liked it when I sat with her like that, as if we were floating on a silvery shimmering lake in a little rowing boat. She could make out the lake perfectly, the smooth surface of the water, the fine sand on the ground and the fish darting about below us and disappearing between long, feathery weeds. She could see it all without closing her eyes, like you see things when you're very little and reality is a big tub full of surprises and you can reach out and touch your imagination. That worried me a bit, because she'd only been able to see the lake with her eyes open for a few days. Before that it was different, before it was just a game, and now I knew she'd soon cross over and get into the rowing boat on her own, while I sat here and listened to her voice.

'You'll have to leave me here this time,' she said.

I didn't want to hear that, and I felt myself starting to cry but I couldn't help it, the tears simply dripped out of my eyes and made dark marks on the white sheet, and I got even more worried about my gran because I realised that she could see the lake perfectly clearly, but not my tears. Her gaze cut through me like a razor blade.

'Promise me one thing,' she said. 'Promise me you won't leave Granddad in the lurch.'

Her thin chest rose and fell quickly, it was so tiring for her to speak. She felt across the sheet for me with one hand. I knew what she meant.

She meant I shouldn't talk, that no one should find out what had really happened on all those afternoons in Granddad's flat.

'Malvina,' she said. 'Promise me.'

I knew she wouldn't be able to die in peace if I didn't do it. So I promised her, and her gaze softened and stayed with me without wandering to the water surface, reaching to the edge of the horizon behind my back.

She died during the night. I dreamed we went out on the water together, me rowing smoothly as if I'd never done anything else in my life, and Gran leaning out at the bow and gliding her fingers through the water.

'Wake me up when we get to the other side,' she said.

***

Lizzy's mother always says you have to make sure for yourself that everything turns out right in your life. There's a lot you can do. You have to make decisions, she says, you have to have the courage to try out new things, you mustn't hide away and you have to put up with set backs. And above all you shouldn't listen to stupid advice, she says with a lopsided grin – meaning you always have to do what you think is right.

I'm not intending to stay for long so I don't lock my bike, I just lean it against the glass-recycling bin. Mrs Bitschek is sitting on the bench but I don't feel like talking. I pretend I haven't noticed her, even ignoring Bratko, who seems to want to make friends with me recently. He rushes upstairs behind me, and I'm surprised how much noise a cat's paws can make on stone. *Tap, tap, tap.* Bratko's not the lithest of cats. He tries to cut off my path to Granddad's front door and ends up precisely between my feet.

'Stupid mog,' I say as he darts down the stairs again, hissing in indignation.

Outside the door, I take a couple of deep breaths. I had a long think yesterday, while my parents were giving me a lecture because of my night in the villa. They didn't believe I'd slept in Anne's bed of course, and they were pretty angry. But I didn't actually care what they said. I was thinking about much more important things. About Granddad and Gran and me. And about how Screwy's going to find everything out soon anyway if we keep seeing each other, and I can feel it in my guts that we will keep seeing each other. I want to see Screwy as much as I can, I thought about that too. What the night with Screwy meant to me and how scared it makes me that it means something to me. All of a sudden I had the feeling I've got something to lose, I do care now what happens to me. It was as if Screwy had burst the bubble with a pin. The soap bubble, that's what I thought of as Dad's mouth moved incessantly; there was nothing but soap bubbles coming out of his mouth, and my soap bubble dissolved into thin air – the space I'd been moving around in for the past few years vanished. And it's all down to Screwy. My thoughts leapt around like crazy, from Granddad to Screwy, then to Gran and Lizzy, and at some point my father said, 'She's not even listening to us.' He planted himself in front of me, placing his hands on the armrests of my chair, and tried to catch my eye. He thought he could intimidate me like that, but it's not so easy to intimidate someone who's just squatted a house, run away from the police and had their first kiss, only a few hours ago.

'No,' I said, 'you're not listening to me.'

And then they were both quiet, and Dad turned away from me, and I had the feeling he knew precisely what I was talking about, I didn't need to say anything more. But I did say something else.

'And that's going to stop,' I said.

Because I'd sorted out my thoughts by then. There was suddenly plenty of room in my head, as if I'd opened a window and let the fresh air come flooding in. Everything was clear. What I have to do. Like Lizzy's mum says: make a decision and then just do it.

Just do it, I think.

The key's in the lock, all I have to do is turn it. I imagine Granddad's in the flat and Gran's ghost as well. That doesn't make things any easier. Maybe Gran's ghost is the worst thing of all. Back then when she died I could feel that she'd gone away, but somehow she was always still with me. Like Lizzy said up in the attic. But she didn't look after me when she was alive, and then when she died she didn't either. She sold me out, because she was too cowardly to defy Granddad, and then she made me promise, and I've been lugging that promise around with me ever since.

That wasn't fair, Gran, I think.

None of it was fair.

I'm here to get rid of that promise. And Granddad. I stand in the corridor for a while. Lukewarm summer air blows in through the window. It's like the other day at the villa – when I leave here I'll never come back. I'll never even set foot across the threshold again. It's just that I don't really feel like saying goodbye right now, I don't need to memorise anything because I won't forget anything anyway. Not the sound of the front door opening, nor Granddad's footsteps on the floorboards, the pictures in the hall, the dust bunnies under the sofa, the smell of old cheese. It's all branded into my memory, I don't have to think for long to summon it up.

It's only when I hear Mrs Bitschek opening the door downstairs that I turn the key in the lock. I have to go in now. I'm even glad that she gives me that nudge, otherwise I'd probably still be standing here tomorrow morning.

'Granddad?' I say cautiously into the dusky light. All the blinds are half-closed. That's unusual, he usually gets up early. People die in bed, he always says. Maybe he's scared of dying, so that's why he reads until late at night and then gets up early, to spend as little time as possible in bed.

Maybe he knows the game's up, I think.

I hear my footsteps on the carpet and the ticking of the kitchen clock.

Maybe he's upped and run away.

I imagine Granddad getting on a train. He has a little brown suitcase with him and he's wearing sunglasses with big dark lenses. As he gets on the train he takes another look around, making sure he's got away unnoticed. He could escape to Guatemala or Brazil, somewhere nobody would look for him. It'd be just like him to run away now, now that I'm here, now that it's all over at last.

But how would he know? I pull up the blinds in the hall, then in the kitchen. There are dirty dishes in the sink and the living room is in darkness too. It's spooky, so I stay in the doorway. From the corner of my eye I notice the record player revolving although the record has long since finished. The speaker is crackling; that used to be the signal to get up, the signal that it was all over. When the speaker started crackling Gran came back in the living room, bringing tea and biscuits and pretending she'd just popped out to the shop round the corner. But she'd been standing in the hall all along. 'A little pick-me-up,' she used to say, and her voice was cheerful, perhaps a tiny bit too cheerful. She put the tea and biscuits down on the living-room table and placed the record player's tone arm back on its rest. When the three of us sat there with tea and biscuits, it all seemed so unreal. It disappeared with the crackling of the speaker, other sounds drowned out the events. Granddad was the Granddad I knew again – the transformation went so quickly, as quickly as his pulse slowed down, his reddened face went pale again. He went into the bathroom. Sometimes he stayed there until someone came to pick me up; it was as if he couldn't look at me. Once he was gone we didn't know what to talk about, Gran and I.

'Granddad?' I say again into the crackling silence.

This time I know what I'm going to say. I don't have to think up any excuses, I don't have to come up with a reason. I'll just say I won't be coming any more from now on and that I won't keep my mouth shut any more. I'll say that as well, that I'm going to talk about it. To Lizzy, to Mrs Bitschek, to Anne and maybe to Screwy. I hope he'll be scared of me, but actually I think he'll try to scare me. They won't believe me, he'll say, and they'll all think I'm crazy. Lizzy won't think I'm crazy and neither will Mrs Bitschek, I'll say.

That stupid Polack, I hear Granddad's voice, she's the one who's crazy!

I know you can talk to the police about it too, but I don't know if I want to yet. Maybe if Lizzy comes with me, if she holds my hand. I've run through the conversations in my mind, from beginning to end. How it started, back then when Granddad came home so drunk, and then every Friday after piano lessons in the bathroom. How he said we were doing it for Gran's sake because Gran can only get better if Granddad's happy too. Maybe they'll want to know what he did. I've read about that, and that you have to answer. I'm scared they'll say it wasn't all that bad. I thought I'd write it all down on a piece of paper, all of the things he did. It's easier to write than to talk.

Number one, I'll write, *he kissed me, on the lips.*

Number two, he touched me, on my breasts and further down.

That sounds stupid, but I can't write about it any better.

Number three, I had to touch him too.

I'll feel dizzy as I push the piece of paper across the table. I haven't written everything down yet, I can't tell them everything yet. I hope there are only women there when I take the piece of paper out of my pocket.

***

Granddad doesn't answer.

I see his shape in the chair ahead of me, his back to the window. He's leaning forwards with his head on the little table he always uses for reading in the evenings. Strips of light fall across his body through the gaps in the blind. At first I think he's asleep. He's nodded off over his books because he's had too much to drink. There's a half-full wine glass and an empty bottle next to his folded arms. Even before I take a step closer, I see the tiny drowned flies floating in the glass. Granddad hates flies in his wine. I don't need to go any nearer to finally realise there's something wrong here.

It makes me feel terrible, but I hope he's dead. He looks dead, or at least not properly alive any more.

Then I run out, feeling the horror at the back of my throat, as if he might get up at any moment and lay his hand on my shoulder.

Mrs Bitschek finds me in the corridor. The door behind me is closed and Bratko is sitting on my lap.

'He might be dead,' I say.

Mrs Bitschek puts her hands on her head.

'Oioioi,' she says, 'oioioi! I didn't think it works so quickly, this time…'

She looks at her hands and crosses herself.

'Holy mother of God,' she says, 'the gift is a burden…'

Then she sits down next to me on the stairs and puts her arm around me. She feels warm and soft, like sinking into an eiderdown.

I'm glad Mrs Bitschek takes charge of everything. She pulls me into her flat and lights white candles, burns sage in the corridor and puts a crucifix around my neck.

'Because of ghost,' she says, 'you must always remember it might be still around, even if the salt works.'

She calls the doctor as well, and my parents, but she doesn't let anyone in.

'No,' she says resolutely when my mother wants to speak to me, 'little bird must sleep, you have done enough bad things already.'

Then she slams the door shut. The bang echoes around the whole building. We hear my parents fussing about in the corridor, my mother's voice very upset.

'What bad things have we done, what?' she says.

I don't think my father says anything, at least I don't hear anything. Mrs Bitschek relays what they're doing, standing at the window with the baby in her arms as I lie on the bench in the kitchen, wrapped in a hundred blankets. She bans me from getting up.

'Stay lying down,' she says when I as much as move a muscle, 'stay lying down and pray.' She makes a grim face as she says it, and I know she's praying.

She's praying that my granddad is dead, but I can't pray, not yet, even though it might be better.

'Mrs Bitschek,' I say, 'you were right.'

She doesn't turn round but I can tell by her shoulders that she winces. She suddenly looks old from behind, bent, not like a forty-year-old but like an ancient old woman.

'Everything you think about my granddad is right,' I say, 'he has an evil spirit, just like Katja's father.'

I pull the blankets up to my nose. My voice sounds muffled like this – I'm not even sure she understands me, but that doesn't really matter. She knows everything anyway, she knew before, and I'm glad she doesn't turn round. It's much easier to say bad things when nobody's looking at you.

An ambulance turns into the yard with flashing blue lights. I see the light darting across the ceiling, and pictures spool through my mind at infinite speed, so fast it scares me. Mrs Bitschek can tell; she puts the baby down and hugs me again, rocking me to and fro. 'Little bird,' she says, 'Katjusha,' and her tears wet my hair. Everything goes quiet, the pictures fly away one after the other, Mrs Bitschek holds me until I'm not scared any more. I'm tired, I've never been so tired in all my life.

'Sleep, little birdy,' says Mrs Bitschek.

Friday

Where the villa used to be, there are piles and piles of rubble. Lizzy and I are sitting at the very top. She's baked me a cake with fourteen candles on it. The cake is all flat and looks sort of like a giant biscuit, because Lizzy only realised afterwards that she'd forgotten to use self-raising flour. She and her mum came back from skiing at one in the morning, just because of my birthday. And it's easy enough to get your flour muddled up at one in the morning. The cake's still delicious. Sort of suspiciously biscuit-like…but I don't say that, I'm much too tactful.

The wind ruffles our hair and blows out the candles.

'Shit,' says Lizzy. 'Now you haven't made a wish.'

I shrug.

'Doesn't matter,' I say.

Then we're both quiet. There's not much left to say. In front of us lie the remains of the villa, the fields, and the time we call the future.

Lizzy picked me up from Mrs Bitschek's this morning, really early, because I wasn't at home and she thought that seemed odd, and she thought my parents seemed odd too. They hummed and hawed on the telephone and didn't want to say where I was. Just that we were having family problems.

'Well,' said my father, 'her granddad's in hospital.'

That's when Lizzy started shouting.

'What the hell's that got to do with Malvina?' she shouted.

And when she got no answer to that, she just carried on shouting, so long and so loud that her mother woke up, and then she talked to my father and found out I was at Mrs Bitschek's.

Five minutes later the two of them were there. Mrs Bitschek made Turkish coffee and sliced Polish yeast cake, and Bratko dropped down from the windowsill onto my lap. It would have been really cosy if so much hadn't happened, and I felt like I was somewhere else again, just not where I really was. We sat together like that for ages, and Mrs Bitschek kicked me under the table, but I couldn't talk. I stared straight ahead at my plate, until Lizzy said:

'Spit it out, Malvina, tell us what's the matter, we're going crazy here.'

When I started telling them my voice was cold, frozen stiff, and I could hear myself talking from a distance. Mrs Bitschek took my hand and every time I had to stop, she pressed my clammy fingers, like spurring on a horse before a jump. I leaped over every fence. I didn't leave anything out; that was hard because I could tell what my words were doing to Lizzy. But I had to talk, to tell the truth, my truth, the way my life really was. By the time I finished Lizzy was crying, and I said:

'It's not that bad.'

As if that could console her, even though I did realise deep down that it is bad.

Now, on top of the pile of rubble, we're both really inhibited. We share the cake like sisters, but between us is a hundred miles of no-man's-land, years when I didn't talk and tried to hide my secret like a dark shadow. How are we ever going to make up that time? My throat cramps with fear that Lizzy might leave. Just leave me sitting here because I didn't tell her the truth right away.

'I'm so angry,' she says suddenly, and I get such a shock I drop the last piece of cake.

'I'm so incredibly angry,' she says, and I can see tears floating in her eyes again.

Dark, furious tears.

I can't get a word out, I can only look at her and wait, wait for her to leave me sitting here because I was such a coward. Other people might not have been such cowards, I think, but maybe a lot of people might have been like me. They might have thought,

I can deal with it, one more day and then another one, I'll tell someone tomorrow or the day after or maybe some day. You don't realise that the secret grows every day. Every hour makes it bigger and harder to speak about.

'I'm so sorry,' I whisper.

Pebbles crumble away under Lizzy's trainers, rolling down the hill.

'You idiot,' says Lizzy roughly. 'Not with you!'

She jumps up, setting off a slight landslide, then she kneels down in front of me, holding onto my legs.

'With me! I'm so incredibly angry with myself,' she says, 'that I didn't notice anything! For so long!'

I can feel myself shaking my head. I can't feel anything else any more, only the thought: Lizzy still likes me, Lizzy's not mad at me.

'I was so scared,' I say. 'That's why I didn't tell you anything.'

I pull Lizzy up before she slides away along with the rest of the hill. She lands roughly on her bum, and we hug again. I don't know how often we're going to have to hug, maybe for hours on end, every day until everything's all right again.

'But I should have noticed,' Lizzy sobs into the small of my neck. 'You're my best friend.'

I don't say anything to that. I didn't give her an opportunity to find out my secret. I encrypted everything so well that in the end I was faced with a whole load of riddles. Lizzy can't help that, not at all.

'I keep thinking of so many things that I only understand now,' she says. 'The way you were so funny when I didn't want to come to your grandparents'. You asked me to come with you once, when I didn't want to. Promise me you'll wait for me at Mrs Neumann's, you said, and I was annoyed. I thought you were just being crazy. I wanted to go swimming instead or somewhere else. I just didn't get it at all.'

'Lizzy, stop it,' I say, 'that's rubbish.'

I wish I could shake her now. I don't do it of course – we hug instead, so hard we almost can't breathe.

'It's not rubbish,' says Lizzy. 'It could all have been over much sooner. And now your granddad's in hospital and we can't do anything. He can't even go to prison as long as he's in hospital.'

Lizzy finds it really hard to deal with injustice like that. It's different with me. I'm glad he's not here any more; I don't care where he is. Maybe one day I'll want him to be punished. But now? Now I'll be happy if everything's fine with Lizzy, I never have to see Granddad again and I can start forgetting. Really forgetting, not burying all the stories in my heart like before. I don't know how that'll work. And that worries me too. I don't know if I'll ever be normal. If I'll ever be able to kiss Screwy without thinking of Granddad and bringing the shadows in my head back to life.

'So what shall we do now?' asks Lizzy.

'Let's go and celebrate, get a Coke and go to the cinema,' I say firmly.

Because it's my birthday today, two times over. Once because it's the first of May, and once because I've finally talked. We'd better get going right away; I pull her up with a tug so she doesn't contradict me. The two of us stumble down the pile of rubble together.

'There's something else I have to tell you,' I say as we get to the bottom.

And I have to do it really quickly, because Screwy's cycling towards us this very minute. He waves from a distance – with both arms, so we can see how well he can ride his bike with no hands.

'Oh no,' Lizzy groans. 'Not him again!'

'Lizzy,' I say, gathering up all my courage, 'I'm in love.'

She looks at me wide-eyed and horrified, then at Screwy, who comes to a stop in a cloud of dust in front of us.

'Not with him,' she hisses at me.

'Sorry,' I whisper. 'It just happened like that.'

'It doesn't just happen!' she whispers back.

Screwy grins. This is just how I imagined them meeting up. Lizzy and Screwy. Oh my God!

'Hi, Lizzy,' he says. 'I'm Malvina's boyfriend.'

Lizzy folds her arms and throws back her head.

'Don't look at me like that,' she says. 'I'm a big girl, I can deal with my best friend going out with an idiot!'

Then a smile sneaks across her face.

'You can come with us if you like,' she says to Screwy in a patronising tone, 'but behave yourself.'

The three of us push our bikes through the tangled grass. Lizzy's jammed the cake tin under her luggage carrier.

'Have I missed something?' asks Screwy, eyeing the cake tin.

'Have you ever!' say Lizzy and I at the same time, looking each other firmly in the eye. Nothing can come between us, that means – nothing and no one.

My name is Malvina and I'm fourteen.

I'm Malvina, the custodian of justice, brave Malvina who always dares to jump, even when you can't see the ground. I jumped, and at the bottom were Lizzy, Screwy, Mrs Bitschek, Lizzy's mum and even Anne. Other people ran away. Paul, for one, and my parents; they were ashamed of what happened. I know I don't have to be ashamed. Lizzy and Screwy showed me how to do it. Every day. They didn't leave me alone for a second.

Some stories don't have a happy ending. Not a big one like in a movie. But there are little things in between, lots of little things that end in a good way. I'll never have to visit my granddad again; he's still too sick but once he's recovered Lizzy's going to get him put in prison with her own two hands. She swore she would on the pile of rubble.

My name is Malvina and I've learned how to shout. I can shout loudly. Sometimes I walk out to where the villa used to be. I climb onto the roof of the supermarket. It's flat, no room for pigeons. It's hot there in summer because the sun reflects off the black tarred roof, and in winter the wind blows snow in your face. I stand right on the edge and stretch out my arms.

Then I shout, so loudly that everyone runs away.

And afterwards I turn round to Screwy.

'How was I?' I ask.

He grins and holds me in his arms. Really tight.